A   NOVEL

MISS ELVA

STEPHENS GERARD MALONE

RANDOM HOUSE CANADA

Published in 2005 by Random House Canada, a division of Random House of
Canada Limited. Distributed in Canada by Random House of Canada Limited.

www.randomhouse.ca

Random House Canada and colophon are trademarks.

LIBRARY AND ARCHIVES CANADA CATALOGUING IN PUBLICATION

Malone, Stephens Gerard, 1957–
Miss Elva / Stephens Gerard Malone.

ISBN 0-679-31339-7

I. Title.

PS8626.A455M58 2005   C813'.6   C2004-905726-X

Book design by Kelly Hill

Printed and bound in the United States of America

10   9   8   7   6   5   4   3   2   1

For Aunt Elva

PART ONE

1927

JANE AT SIXTEEN was all flaming youth and cheek-bones. Bold to her betters some'd say, mostly Rilla, by way of apologizing for her daughter. Jane would never be sorry for a goddamned thing, but Jesus! That girl could turn the head of a stone angel.

Now you didn't usually see her kind in Demerett Bridge, Mi'kmaq had their place up in Indian Brook, but Rilla had that thing going with her white man Amos so you couldn't very well say no. And Jane? Half white so no one minded her checking herself out in windows up and down Commercial Street on account of her good half being on the outside. So, Girl don't you be giving me any business, was all she'd get from King Duplak for sassin' him and saying she'd make that ol' catalogue dress and wouldn't buy it in his shitty five-and-dime even if she could. She ripped the page right out of the T. Eaton book and slipped it into her pocket so she could paste it on her mirror.

Rilla was searching through cans on the shelf and Duplak said, Hey now, it took the wife some time to get them all facing right like. So Rilla counted out nickels, going red at the cheeks 'cause she'd been caught looking for cheaper prices in behind. Be glad when this strike's over, Mr. Duplak.

Christ, she's going to want this on account, King was thinking, knowing full well what no rails coming off the foundry lines meant. Wouldn't be enough for Amos Stearns to feed his harem over there on Kirchoffer Place, specially since he'd been off sick. Amos'd been the security man at the foundry, sort of like a policeman with a lot more hitting power, but what good was that if you had to spend half your day in the crapper? When Amos's poor stomach became a regular thing, there was talk of a pension or something, then the manager, Urban Dransfield—who everyone in

Demerett Bridge now hated because of the strike—
said, Thank you very much you can't work any more
here's a watch with your name on it.

That was before the strike, and now, not so many
potatoes for the stew pot. No paycheques in a town con-
trolled by the Maritime Foundry Corporation meant
Amos'd been unable to meet ends with the boarders in
that place of his. Must be why his old lady was back on
the road. King'd seen for himself Stearns's Mi'kmaq
whore in that old Ford of his. Heard she was doing
washing as far north as Raven River for those German
yahoos up there. Hey, honest folks were hurting too and
thank Jesus they'd rather starve before swabbing out
skivvies and bedsheets for River people. Yeah, right. If
washing was all she was doing. King smiled, remembering the old days when Rilla wasn't looking so hard-
ridden. Why if it wasn't for the wife out back, he'd show
Amos's squaw his own laundry shed.

He counted each coin again. Didn't matter that the
woman had been a customer for over thirteen years.
It's not like she was Stearns's legal wife. Indians got no
credit no how, so Jane didn't need a new dress and
no, added Rilla, you're not getting your hair bobbed
either.

Daylight flooded through the open door catching
the dust unawares. Barely reaching the latch, Harry
had shadowed Rilla and her girls into the store. He was
too young to be captivated by Jane's adolescent charms

or to know he shouldn't stare at the other sister, well, half-sister, the one who wasn't as pretty as Jane. Normally the ugly one sat out on the front porch when she came into Demerett Bridge shopping with her ma and Jane. Sometimes she'd colour with chalk on a writing tablet. Once when she did it, Harry stopped carving his name in backwards letters into the steps of his dad's pool hall across the street, came over and looked. Said she couldn't draw and why didn't she draw boats? He might like them better if she did boats, but the girl, Elva, just said, Go away. She didn't sit outside today because there were men on the corner, shouting now, looking to make trouble for someone new around these parts.

Elva had trouble breathing on hot days or when she got herself worked into a lather, so when she turned away from the window and said, You have to help him, it came out all huffy.

Rilla stared at the Elva girl. What was she thinking, giving orders to Mr. Duplak?

Jane flipped another page in the catalogue. Big deal. It wasn't like anyone was going to take notice of *her*. "Help who and stop that wheezing."

It took ages for Elva to get out, "There's a man on top of the clock. Went up it like a caterpillar. He's jabbing it with an army knife."

How could he do that and hold on to the clock? Jane wanted to know, but more men were tumbling out of the pool hall and crowding around the clock so Elva didn't say. They were grey and furry like rats, Elva said and added, "There's no more poison and there's rats in the cellar."

Jane reached over and pinched her arm.

"Don't!"

"What's he doing now?" Mr. King Duplak came over to the window to see for himself.

The pole sitter was showing the others a silver timepiece, one of those really old-fashioned watches on a fob that used to sway like a garland across fancy waistcoats. From the window where she watched, standing on her toes to be as tall as Jane, Elva guessed the watch had once been broken and maybe he'd repaired it. Probably thought he could set the town clock too. Some people are born that way. Wanting to fix things even when they don't want fixin', only the man no one had never seen in Demerett Bridge before didn't know about the clock being sacred and you don't touch it.

"Is he cute?" Jane asked.

"He's kind of pasty and he wears funny glasses but he's dreamy."

Jane was always saying dreamy this or dreamy that, so lately *dreamy* was Elva's favourite word. Then she got all short for breath again when the men outside starting throwing rocks.

"He'll fall and break his glasses!"

Stephens Gerard Malone

"Show's over," said Mr. Duplak, drawing the blinds. The town clock hadn't kept time since the hurricane of '04, and according to King Duplak, he'd no business up there in the first place. The rusting timepiece was a tribute of sorts, but less to the Nova Scotian town surviving the storm and more to the prevailing Scottish thriftiness that didn't see the need to pay for a monument when a perfectly useless clock would do.

"Pink-whiskered Jesus! Like a pack of dogs been through here! Who's going to clean that?"

It hadn't been enough for li'l Harry Winters to follow Elva into the store and stare at her. No. He had to go to the counter for a penny jawbuster, then wander over to the corner where he stood wide-eyed and sucking, oblivious to the trail of black muck from his shoes. Goddamned tar ponds! A mecca for boys of Harry's age, wanting to throw stuff in, or worse, drag dead things out. Now Harry's cub-like marks were everywhere.

Jane said, Haw haw, when she saw the mess on His Lordship's floor.

Only Elva saw the footprints as something more than an hour with a brush and bleach, taking some doing to scrub out the wooden planks. A tar map. Their long crescent harbour was right there, on the floor of Duplak's store, Demerett Bridge at the far northeastern end with Ostrea Lake in behind, the foundry, the black ponds and the monastery about halfways, and just a little to the southeast, Kirchoffer Place, where the factory

8

workers lived and where Elva's ma ran her man's boarding house. Not that she'd learned about maps in school, Elva didn't go. Gil taught her about maps. But his maps were drawn in sand.

Where do you think Gil is? she might have asked Jane, but Elva didn't want her sister to think she'd been forgiven for killing her pet bird and as it was, Elva had a hard time remembering she wasn't talking to Jane. Gil and his brother, Dom, were two years older than Jane, although Elva hadn't seen Gil for so long now, not since he'd run off, that if it weren't for Dom, she'd forget what Gil looked like.

It used to be that on Sunday mornings after church in Demerett Bridge, the brothers, free from starchy collars and wearing only torn-off dungarees in summer, drifted down to the end of Kirchoffer Place where the road tinkled with loose slate and ran off to the beach because, maybe, Jane would be there. If she was so inclined, they were not disappointed. Elva could always be counted on to be waiting.

Before they got a few years older and just sat around on washed-up logs moaning, There's nothing to do in this armpit of a province, and, Can't wait to get out, Gil would etch maps in the sand with a piece of sand dollar, all of them planning the afternoon's adventure. Usually it ended up being to Corry Canyon, where there was a stonecutter's hut and everyone knew the Indians had scalped him and left the hut in ruins.

Don't be so foolish, Rilla said about that.

No one got tired of going out there, but organizing it was sometimes a battle. Dom would kick out the map with his foot, saying, No, stupid, that's wrong, it's over here! Gil'd say, Fuck off! His French accent made Elva giggle. Jane'd watch the two boys getting all sweaty against each other as if she was deciding something, but what, Elva never figured. A plan agreed to, they'd be off, running, whooping, jumping lupins if it was June, leaving Elva quickly distant, crying, Wait!

If anyone slowed down, that would be Gil. But like it was said, Gil had been away for ages and Dom was busy now, on the Lord's day.

"He followed *her* in here," King was saying, pointing to Elva, "and she's your problem." Harry had already hightailed it back to his dad's pool hall, the most prudent course of action, but King wasn't about to let Rilla do the same.

Now he was calling for reinforcements from out back: Bernice, the wife. An unpleasant piece of work, her. Stuck up like a Woolworths heiress and didn't say much. Fishy lips with whiskers and from Cape Breton. Made a better Bernie than Bernice. She sounded odd to Elva because her mother tongue was Gaelic; it left the woman spitting a lot of extra vowels she didn't know what to do with. Figured her old man was way too kind letting Rilla and her half-breeds in amongst their rough, unpainted wooden shelves and pine plank floors that coughed up summer dust whenever anyone with boots walked upon them, tinkling with vibrating crockery. The Emporium, as Mrs. La-de-da Bernice liked to call it. Jane always made a face when she said la-de-da.

Christ, Rilla wanted to say, except Rilla'd cut her own tongue out before she'd take the Lord's name in vain. Forgive me, Father. It was for Jane's sake that she even considered swearing, but what choice was there? Rilla still had to drive out to Raven River that afternoon and there was no way she could have supper late— Amos wouldn't tolerate that. Jane would have to get the evening meal on the table.

"Get on with you, straight home, girl. Put the turnips on to boil and stay out of his way."

Amos had to be fed. Christ!

Elva was told to go with Mrs. Duplak and find a pail.

"No. I want to go with Jane."

Jane'd have none of that. Neither would Rilla. Elva sensed her mother didn't like to go to creepy Raven River on her own, especially if it was starting to get dark on the way back. As for Jane, well, Elva knew Jane didn't want her kid sister following her anytime. Let's see, time with her mother, who wanted her, or with Jane, who didn't. When no one noticed, and who noticed Elva, she stepped into one of Harry's tar patches and said, Oh look, I have it on my shoe, too.

Rilla set her meagre bag of groceries on the counter like it was filled with rocks. This would have been her third *Christ!* of the afternoon.

Get off the two of you and no shilly-shallying, Rilla warned, but no one heard because Jane on her own with a mind of her own was already out the door trying to lose Elva. That wouldn't do in a town full of idle men frustrated by a long strike, bored and looking for laughs. Hopefully it wouldn't last, the bit about Jane's own mind, that is. At least Rilla didn't need to worry about Miss Elva. Blessed be small mercies. Misshapen. Miss Ugly. Miss Nothing.

"It's hot." Jane was swinging back and forth, her hands clasped around an old fence post. Then she was off, and not in the direction of home. That was the arse out of her mother's stricture.

When Elva took her place, closed her eyes and clasped her hands around the post, she was sure she could feel where Jane's hands had been, warm like. Maybe even magical, for Elva could believe it really was she, and not Jane, greeting the spring sun, stretching for coolness against the sea wind, that wind blowing through her long, oily black hair, pressing Rilla's made-over dress against her long legs, her nipples tingling underneath the slippery fabric with every gulp of salt air.

But spells don't last forever. When brightness washed away her dreams and Elva blinked to see Jane jump across the ditch to the road, the fingers clutching the post in front of her were gnarled and twisted, knobby like sandpipers caught in the ooze of the foundry's tar ponds until they were nothing more than limpid black lumps. In the wake of Jane, Elva became the short, ugly thing she was, shoulders drooping like late-summer sunflowers. It's like the good Lord was rushed, slapped down her noggin, gave it a yank and short-shrifted her on a neck, her aunt Blanche had sighed with a sadness when Elva was born, and echoed in some way or another every time she visited Rilla. It was left to Elva to punctuate that with a tiny *oh!*

"Well, what are you going to do with the money?"

Nothing got past Jane. Must have heard the quarter fall out of Elva's birthday note from Auntie Blanche and go *blonk!* on the kitchen floor before Elva scooped it up and hid it in her change purse. Jane'd been trying to part it from her sister ever since.

Bus coming, with a frisky churn of dust and gravel.

And of course, Jane believed that Elva was being plain hateful by not sharing her birthday bounty. Hadn't Jane been saying for weeks to anyone who'd listen that she'd die if she didn't see *The Flaming Forest* and it was only going to be at the Towne movie palace for a week?

"It's got flappers, you know, and Mounties and savage Indians."

Normally, Elva would've given Jane anything. Funny how that went, the snottier Jane was, the more

Elva wanted to do for her. But not this time. Jane wasn't getting that money and both sisters knew why.

"It's that stupid bird, isn't it?"

"You know," said Elva.

The bus hurtled by, causing Jane to step onto the shoulder and shield her eyes from the grit, so she missed the passengers' faces through ashen-shaded windows. Behind it came an automobile. Now there was something you didn't see in Demerett Bridge every day and it demanded that the girls pause. This one had rolling rounded fenders, one dented, and a yellow cloth roof. In the moment between the clearing of the cloud from the bus and the passing car, Elva caught the flash of dark glasses, low hat, paisley scarf.

The silence of the country road back around them, Jane had no intention of filling it with an old argument. "I could do that, and be in the movies. Everyone says I could." What was the word they used on the radio? Jane wrapped her hands in front of her chest as if she were revealing the Sacred Heart of Jesus.

"Emoting," Elva said. Emoting was Hollywood lingo for making loopy faces to a camera for lots of money.

"Yes, better at that. Everyone says so. Watch." The accompanying grimace might have meant a heart severed by love's inconstancy, or merely the need to belch.

So by rights, didn't Jane just have to see for herself by going to the movies? She stomped her foot. That was to let Elva know she was serious.

Who's everyone? Elva wanted to know, fingering the quarter through her faded calico purse. She liked it because it looked like a kitten with a silver comb in its back.

There was enough for two matinee tickets, maybe some Milk Duds too. Caramel centres were Elva's favourite because they'd melt in between your teeth, saving some for later, even if going to the movies meant she had to sit in that really hot last-row balcony with the other Mi'kmaq where she couldn't see very well and couldn't hear over the clicking of the projector. But Rilla had said the coin was to be Elva's mad money, you know, for a girl's emergencies and hidden in her sock when out with a fella so he'd never know you had it. That way she'd always have a way home.

"Like you'll need that," said Jane. "Don't share, then. I don't care." Not that she had any intention of bringing Elva with her.

The now distant bus lurched off the Old Narrows Road and rocked its way into the centre of Demerett Bridge. Elva didn't care for buses. They reminded her that sometimes people left you. That Jane might be one of them. It never occurred to her that someone might want to come back.

Jane cut off the road and hopped the fence beyond the ditch. So what if she showed her panties doing it.

"Hey! Where're you going?"

"None of your beeswax."

"Rilla said take me right home—"

"Then go, you baby-la-la, get home and start dinner and don't say!"

Jane was heading in the direction of the monastery but it wasn't going to be any business of Elva's as to why.

"I'll tell her about the milk. I've seen you."

Elva had to yell that to be heard, but it stopped her sister. Stopped her dead in her tracks. Jane turned, eyes wide, teeth set. Uh-oh. Elva had seen that look before.

"You spying little witch! Tell, then! But don't think I won't twist your arm off."

Jane bent Elva's arm sharply until she cried, but that was the end to it.

"What'll you do if they find out about the milk?"

At first Jane told Elva to shut her mouth, then, "Someday I'll make enough to buy a ticket to Halifax, maybe even New York. And never come back. So who cares if they know?"

Her mother had spent a life scrubbing other people's floors and for what? Never been anywhere. Not Jane. She'd get out of Demerett Bridge. She'd never get on her hands and knees for any man like Rilla did for that Amos Stearns. And she was going to be famous.

"Where will you get money?"

Jane just twirled and tossed and smiled. Like it could be done.

Sure it could, going off to seek your fortune in the big city. Didn't Elva know someone who did just that?

Gil? So long ago by now that she stopped hoping he'd come back, even if it was more apt to say he was a boy running away from home after everyone said he cut his father's legs off. Well, not as if Gil held the knife, he was only thirteen at the time, but he might as well have. That's what Amos and even Gil's own mother had said, when Gil fell asleep on night watch five years ago, letting the *Meghan Rose* hit that shoal. They had to cut Mr. Barthélemy's legs off after they got tangled and crushed in the schooner's rigging. Elva'd miss Jane if she left, but she herself had tried to leave once and the aborted attempt proved to Elva she had no want to go anywhere.

And this was why. Following Jane through the acres of silvery grass, she came to her disappearing place. It was by that porkchop-like lake of salt water behind the town, leaking in from the sea, wrapping itself around and then bleeding off into the foundry's tar ponds. Along the way, Ostrea Lake paid a call at the shores of the monastery. There, if she lay among the reeds filling the void between the harbour and the lake, ripe with strawberries by early June, dragonflies buzzing ferociously over her head, the sun would melt Elva into sweet dreams, into nothing, into being Jane.

"Won't Mr. Barthélemy need legs in heaven?"

Spring grass, minty green, already waist high, was brushing Elva's open fingers.

"Nope. He's in hell."

But won't Gil's father need them there, too? Elva wondered but didn't say. They had come to the monastery gates and she asked Jane if it was okay to go in, it being only Friday and not a church day. Jane said, Who cares about a couple of girls, so shut up.

The iron hinges winced as Jane boldly entered the Eye, the centre of the Franciscan order's compound, the self-proclaimed spiritual epicentre of Demerett Bridge. When most of the seaside town buckled under the 1904 hurricane, coincidentally days after the Brothers condemned the opening of Winnie McClelland's House of Burlesque as a godless vice the citizens would answer to God for, the eye of the storm passed over the cemetery by the monastery, leaving it untouched. The Franciscans liked to say the Eye of God had blessed the dead as a lesson to the living.

Now you'd think from the way folks still went on about it, and from the look of a town best described as saggy, that the hurricane had only just happened, and not ten years before Elva was born. By the waterfront, wooden sidewalks railed like roller-coaster rides, storefronts disintegrated into windborne straw, and flooding turned streets into soupy canals. Even the bridge across the creek that drained Ostrea Lake into the sea, and for some reason needed to be appended to the name of the town, had been blown away, and never was replaced. The Demerett family, the town's first, had built the bridge to the grassy knoll by the lake where they liked to picnic. Rich folks from the olden days, before they got all petty about paying income taxes, did those sorts of philanthropic things, especially if they got their names on a plaque. While they once owned a slew of smart houses behind Commercial Street and along the waterfront, the only Demeretts left in town were enjoying heavenly favour in the Eye.

The other structure unscathed by the storm was that damned theatre, where the evening show with the Fan Fan Girls and Jimmie the Talking Dog went on as scheduled—well, the troupe had come all the way from Toronto and was not to be missed—with patrons ferried for a nickel in a dory through flooded streets. Following fashion, the House of Burlesque would reinvent itself in a few years as a nickelodeon, then as the Towne Theatre, the *e* added for class. No pronouncement from the pulpit was ever made as to what its longevity meant.

The Brothers' living quarters in the monastery was a reclining two-storey stone house, serving to barricade one side of the Eye. The tar ponds, effluent from Demerett Bridge's largest, and now strike-bound, employer, the Maritime Foundry Corporation, maker of all things railroad, blackened another. To the south, tombstones were hemmed in by an iron grape-leaf gate. A squat stable, used for storage, completed the rudimentary square.

Jane was well on into the yard. Walked right over graves, she did. Elva tried to dodge the mounds and said, Sorry, when she couldn't. She guessed where Jane was going. The legless body with the hole in the head was all anyone in town or at home was talking about, although Elva had no desire to see for herself. She wished Jane didn't either, but Elva'd thrown her lot in with her sister and she'd follow it through, if she could keep up. Besides, she didn't want to be the one to face Amos if Jane and Rilla weren't home when he expected.

Alphonse Barthélemy was to be buried next day in the narrow strip of potter's field between the cemetery and the tar pond because, as Rilla's priest had explained, the man was in mortal sin. Saturday was the only day the burial could take place, Father Cértain said, it being an unholy Jew day and good enough for burying bad Catholics. Unfortunately, Alphonse blew his head off after Sunday's mass, so the corpse was bound in coal sacks from the mill and kept on ice slabs in the stable for over five days.

But that's where we keep cool the Halifax-bound cheese, some of the Brotherhood had protested to their spiritual authority. To make matters worse, Alphonse had missed, blowing away his jaw, before he was successful with a second shot. His widow couldn't afford a coffin, and no amount of coal sacks could stop the blood from seeping onto the floor. And everybody knows blood drips from a suicide can be heard from miles away as a warning to everyone else. That pearl of wisdom came courtesy of Aunt Blanche, who had words of wisdom for all occasions. Jane had to see for herself.

From watching the Brothers from her bedroom window on the other side of the tar pond, Elva knew a sexton usually worked the cemetery, raking leaves, setting stones, tossing out the flowers that inevitably showed up in violation of the strict no-clutter rule. Apparently, not today.

"Where is everyone?"

Jane didn't care. Eating? Praying? Whipping themselves so they didn't dream about women's breasts? Elva was starting to wheeze again so Jane shushed her with a splash of green water from the wall fountain. It pissed out of the mouth of a woman's face that had been chipped away in case any of the monks got ideas. The fountain had an upper bowl for people that drained into a lower bowl for cats and dogs, and the water always looked brackish so Elva said, Don't!

They threaded their way through the mossy headstones to the stable, Elva the only one worried by the nearby casements, certain dozens of eyes were staring from them, fingers pointing, especially when Jane helped herself to a small shovel left by an open grave. When they reached the back of the red-tiled stable, Jane unhesitatingly jerked the handle of the shovel into the glass, stifling Elva in mid-wheeze.

"Don't you start that! You wanted to come. Get in there and open the door."

But Elva knew there was a dead man inside and, What if the devil is in there too with all those dead babies because the devil has them if they're not baptized?

That meant nothing to Jane. Death was too abstract to mean squat. She dragged Elva close and, easily picking her up, boosted her through the broken panes. Elva clung to Jane's neck, avoiding the sharp splinters around the sill, then dropped to the floor on the other side.

"Now open the door!"

Years of accumulated grime on the rows of glass squares diffused sunlight over squat cylinders of cheese stacked with mathematical neatness, going sweet. Elva huddled against the wall but no way was she going to look. Then a whisper, like an animal noise, came from the corner.

"El-va?"

The voice was weary but *dreamy*. The memory of that whisper would dog Elva for years, rattling around inside her like the sea in a shell, always accompanied with the recollection of ripening milk. A strange way for the ghost of Alphonse Barthélemy to appear.

But the day when this terror became a sweet dream was a long ways off. A shadow darted against the lower window. Something was brushing against her leg, sniffing and cold and wet. Elva scratched the coolness of the dirt floor against her palms as she pushed herself up towards the door, away from whatever was circling her, words struggling out in bits and pieces as she fumbled with the latch, until something too solid for a ghost gathered her from behind, enclosing her in wiry arms.

"Sweet jumpin' Jesus, Elva! Not so much noise!"

Whoever it was smelled as strong and familiar as a man who had laboured a long day. Jane's pounding against the outside door matched that from inside Elva's chest, racing up to inside her head. He wrapped his arm around her face to quiet her while he pulled back the door latch and flooded the stable with light. Jane blinked, amazed, until the man dragged her inside, shutting the door behind them all. Only then did Elva's ghost release his temporal grip. A dog, slick black with brown eye patches, wagged his tail by his side.

"Domenique!"

He pulled a cigarette from his shirt pocket, lit it and had it bouncing on his lips. The habit was new but he made it seem old.

"It's not Dom, you idiot," Jane said.

"Can't fool you?"

"Never. Besides, you're thinner now than he is."

Not a word from him in five years and yet Jane could still tell Guillaume and Domenique Barthélemy apart in a heartbeat. Gil, like his twin brother, not overly tall, square of face, maybe even plain. And some people think the ocean is just water. Dom's face expressed calm, reflecting an inner peace, 'cause he's close to God. Or so his maman, Jeanine, claimed. Gil was different. A funnel cloud just itching to form into a twister. Jane said Gil had an undertow and it could suck you down if you weren't careful.

But you've come back!

Gil smiled and traced his finger around Elva's face. "And you, my little marionette?"

Don't do that, don't look at me. And Elva turned away.

He took her chin in his hand and pulled it towards him. "You still do that?"

Of course she did. What did Gil expect? What did any of them know? Elva certainly hadn't forgotten it. Or him. How could she? Sure, it was just a comb, an old comb with some of its teeth missing. But Gil had remembered it was her birthday. Dom didn't think about those things, and in later years, Elva'd attribute Dom not being considerate like Gil to his being busy with God's work and all. Like everyone said, that was more important.

The comb thing happened on Elva's seventh birthday. Jane, for her last birthday, had laid in the groundwork for her party weeks in advance, humming *Hap-py-loo-loo to me*, getting chafed in the hands scrubbing dishes without complaint, leaving out the flour tin on the table, even managing to be nice to Amos. The result, apart from Amos slipping Rilla fifty cents and telling her to get that girl something, if only to shut her up, was a tray of cupcakes from Rilla. Elva had seen them on top of the icebox. Vanilla, with cocoa and cinnamon sprinkles on yellow icing. Yellow was Rilla's favourite colour. Too bad Elva spilt tea at dinner and Amos said, Get out of my sight. She hated that she was always spilling things because that meant the closest Elva would come to those cupcakes was dreaming about them. But sometime during the night she awoke, like someone had shaken her. Elva hadn't even noticed that Jane had crawled in beside her and was asleep. There on the side table in all its glory was a single radiant cupcake on one of Rilla's best tea saucers. Elva would never know who put it there, surely not Jane, but she held it in her hands and stared at it for a full five minutes before she pinched off little pieces and let them melt in her mouth. She didn't expect the same fuss for her own birthday, but she was secretly hoping someone would remember.

Amos said nothing to Elva on his way out to the foundry that morning. Rilla said, Happy birthday, Elva, and put her arms around her and kissed her head. Jane was sitting at the table eating toast and looking like she'd swallowed something that was tickling the inside of her tummy. No presents. No cupcakes on top of the icebox. Elva pulled her longest face ever as she sat down, too disappointed to eat.

Rilla didn't like her girls to be around when the boarders came down for breakfast, so she hurried them along as she began to spoon out the eggs onto a row of plates. That's when Jane leaned over to her sister and said that Gil and Dom were waiting for them.

Really? She was being invited to spend the day with Jane and Gil and Dom, not running after them all like an afterthought? A genuine, honest to goodness, you're coming too? To hell with breakfast! Elva beamed. Best present ever!

The boys were waiting in Dorion's field that had been left fallow, next to the Barthélemy farm. It was already thick with spring clover. Dom was looking for the elusive four leaves. Gil was holding nets attached to long poles and gave one to Elva. His father used them to scoop minnows for bait and would skin him alive if he knew he'd taken them.

"What for?"

Gil said Dom had a school project so they were hunting for mourning cloak butterflies.

"I found one!" Dom studied the clover, then gave it to Jane.

Jane was picking off the four leaves, one by one. Oh Jane, said Dom. As Gil had only brought three nets, it was a given that she'd not been doing any work.

"They're kinda black with white trim and little purple dots," said Gil. "But they're hard to come by and Dom'll get a full ten points if we find one."

Nobody expected Elva to catch anything. Jane said with that gimpy arm of hers she'll scare everything from here right into town.

"I will not," said Elva, and she tried her best to follow Gil and Dom, swinging her net after anything that moved.

Jane quickly got bored watching everyone run about for butterflies, and when Dom saw her sit in the clover and start weaving headbands from the mauve flowers, he set down his net beside her.

Elva's breath caught.

"What is it?"

She was too excited to speak, to do anything but point. Gil laughed and took her net from her.

"Elva, you've done it! You've got a mourning cloak here! Dom! Jane! Elva got one!"

When the others joined them, Gil held up Elva's net. Dom beamed as he opened his knapsack and took out a block of wood, a long darning pin stuck into it. Gil reached into the net and very gently secured the flapping butterfly in his fingers.

"What are you doing?"

"I'm going to mount it," Dom said.

"No! You're going to kill it!"

"C'mon, Elva. It's just a bug."

When Jane noticed her tears she said, "Couldn't you put it in a jar or something?"

"Yes! In a jar, but don't hurt him!"

Everything was a him to Elva.

"What's the matter with you?" Dom said. "It's a butterfly."

"Yes, Elva," said Jane. "It's just a butterfly."

She let out a holler when it looked as if the pin was going to be driven home.

"Look, Dom," said his brother. "Maybe not, eh? Let it go."

"You know how hard these are to come by?"

"Just let it go."

No way, and Dom made again to pin the insect to the wood. He would have succeeded had his brother not suddenly let it go.

"Yes, Gil!" said Elva.

He smiled at her, not seeing Dom fire up quickly and swing his knapsack, catching him in the face. Gil went down hard, and his brother stormed off home.

"Sorry, Elva. It being your birthday and all."

She said it was okay, but the day was ruined.

Gil was twelve when this happened and still a year away from crewing on the *Meghan Rose*. Amos was always saying about people like the Barthélemys, Don't have two cents to rub together, that kind. Well, Gil didn't have two cents for anything, let alone Elva's birthday, but he'd found the comb in the patch of grass with the war cenotaph on it, next door to the Towne movie palace. Guess he thought now was as good a time as any to give it to her.

"Sorry, Elva." He pulled it out of his back pocket, broken when he fell. He looked again after his brother. "Now you've got two instead of one."

It was the most beautiful thing Elva had ever seen, even if it was smashed. A woman's comb like the one Rilla used to pull up her hair behind her head. Only this one was shiny and full of colours like it was made from a rainbow. All Elva could do was hold the pieces in her hand and say, *oh!*

Gil was suddenly embarrassed and not sure where to look.

Elva wanted to put them in her hair right there, but Jane grabbed the broken comb out of her hand.

Hey now, said Gil. Elva started to cry.

"Why'd you do that?"

Jane thought about being penitent.

"Because she'd want to take it up to her room and sit by the mirror and put it in. Then she'd see."

"See what?"

"That she's ugly and she's better off not having pretty combs in her hair."

But that's not what hurt the most for Elva. That came next when Gil said, "I wasn't thinking. You keep it, then."

"Me? What do I want with some broken old thing you found?"

A gift too pretty for some, not fit for others. And only Elva remembered why she turned her face away.

"Why are you back now?" Jane asked, tucked in the gloom of the ripe stables.

"Heard my old man was dead. Figured there'd be a do."

"You won't be welcome."

"So? I know what people think of me."

"I hope you stay." Elva had spoken very quietly, so it was doubtful she'd been heard.

"Well, don't worry. I'll stay long enough to make some money, get me out of Nova Scotia. Then the Major and I are gone for good." Gil stooped to scratch his dog's head. "He adopted me in Halifax. Figure he'll look out for me at sea."

"Don't you know about the strike?"

"There's always work."

"Not now. Unless you want to, scab."

He shrugged off the dirty word.

"Jane wants to see blood," Elva suddenly said, finding her voice, wanting Gil to see her.

If Jane's look could speak it'd say, Shut up!

Gil took no offence and led them deep into the shed. Elva didn't care for the smell of things.

"Is that him?" Jane was whispering.

Gil nodded at the short bundle on the work table. "What's left of him."

Not much to see in the dusty, opaque gloom. Could have been anything wrapped up there. Bit of a disappointment.

"Is John still the sexton?"

Both of the girls nodded.

"It'll be okay if I sleep here tonight. John won't mind. And when it's dark, I'll soak the old man in tar from the pond and light him. Ought to fire up like a torch, a human torch."

"You wouldn't!" But Jane sounded hopeful.

It was not lost to Elva that Jane was touching Gil's arm.

"Dom and Father Cértain have arranged —"

"The bastard's better off in the pond. Save Maman the cost of burying 'im."

You didn't always think like that.

"It'll put off your mother, you coming back." Jane's eyes were riveted to the coal-dust-stained funeral shroud, as were Elva's. The air was getting sweeter, sickly sweet.

"Still down on her knees, praying for Dom to be pope?"

Jane's face clouded.

Uh-oh. Foul mood acoming. Lately, all it took was saying stuff about Dom.

"And my good brother obeys her in all things?"

Jane shrugged.

The air, thought Elva, so sweet, so thick.

Gil patted the swathed corpse. "Too bad you'll miss your own party, Pappa."

And Elva vomited quietly into her hands.

"Elva, you thing!"

The fresh air, the sound of water trickling into that fountain, was a godsend. Or was it that she had leaned her head against his shoulder when Gil picked her up and carried her outside that made her feel better?

I always knew you'd come back.

Jane followed. "You can't stay in there and you can't go to town. No one's forgotten about the wreck. What your father did to himself, it's bringing it all back."

"You mean, the lies?"

Wiping her hands on the grass, Elva added that the striking men in town were scratching for a fight. Rilla said that's what men do when they're drunk and don't have work. That's why they threw stones at the guy fixing the clock.

Gil chuckled. "Someone tried to fix that old relic?"

"Some fool," said Jane.

"Who?"

Elva shrugged. "Never saw him before. Black and starchy like an undertaker."

"And white," added Jane.

"White? Fixing the clock?"

A bell pealed from somewhere inside the Brothers' residence.

"I gotta go."

"Where?"

"Nothing," he said, kind of confused, searching the direction of Demerett Bridge.

They followed Gil, bending over to hide below the tombstones in case anyone was watching from the windows. At the gates, they parted.

Rilla would be back from Raven River soon and supper still hadn't been started. They both knew what Amos would be like should his meal be late.

"I hate him," Jane cursed quietly.

So do I, thought Elva, but as it was in regards to her own father, she didn't say it out loud. But she did say, "I'm glad Gil's back."

"He didn't come for you."

Reluctantly they left the Eye and followed the shore of the tar ponds around to Kirchoffer Place, Elva periodically looking over her shoulder to see the young man diminish into nothing.

Rilla was cleaning up from the evening meal in the summer kitchen of the boarding house that had come to Amos from his late wife, Dorothy; Dotsie, as he came to call her. A woman thirteen years his senior and a widow, she owned the boarding house on Kirchoffer Place when Amos started with the foundry. Amos, walking all the way from his home in Canso to look for work, needed a place to hang his hat, and Dotsie had rooms. His subsequent rise through the factory ranks paralleled his fast track from the bed in room number five to Dotsie's own. Matronly, somewhat prone to worry, Dotsie died less than a year after they were married. Although in the months before her death she ate herself to hot-air balloon proportions and developed a clumsiness that left her bruised all over, no one thought anything amiss of her sudden personality change prior to her abrupt passing, or how Amos had quickly come into real estate. If there was room in her coffin now, she'd be spinning at the notion of a Mi'kmaq woman taking her bed, in her house.

Don't say shitty, was all Rilla said about spending the afternoon on her knees scrubbing floors.

Elva, rebuked, crossed her arms, immovable on the point. It wasn't fair to Rilla and yes it was shitty. And besides, if Jane was allowed to say shitty, how come she wasn't?

The wall of screens, their only defence against horse-flies mean as starving beggars, rattled in the sea air.

"He wouldn't have made you clean that up if —"

"If what, girl?"

"We were white."

"You'd do well to be silent 'bout that." Rilla stretched the kink of a long day out of her back. When she did that she always said, Cold in my kidneys. "God is fair, girl; men are not."

Her mother might as well have said, You be thankful, Elva, for what the good Lord provides, you don't hear the birds minding what table crumbs they get.

But I'm not a bird.

Hard to accept that leftovers were her only due and, oh yeah, thanks God. *He's fair, is He?* All Elva had to do was look in the mirror and see just how fair God had been to her when every day she was reminded how much

He'd given Jane. Still, it didn't matter to Elva, well, not so much, that Rilla preferred Jane. That was like gracing a table with a centrepiece of mayflowers instead of stinkweed. Purely natural to go for what was pleasing.

Rilla groaned through clenched teeth as she strained with the heavy bucket of soapy water to the screen door and poured it down the steps where it foamed into the sand. For Rilla's sake, Elva now regretted what she'd done to get out of going with her. It needled her sharply. Guess whatever makes Jane beautiful and impervious to pain left me deformed and weak of heart, she thought, so weak that every hurt rushes in and unpacks.

Elva might have had a delicious afternoon in Raven River with Rilla all to herself even if it did mean visiting bloody krauts who fed their horses in the last war with girlie guts. Well, that's what Amos said.

Amos also believed that Germans hereabouts, any Germans, must have been spies in the war and were behind the *Imo* and *Mont Blanc* colliding in the harbour and blowing the crap out of Halifax in '17. Elva was only three when that happened, but Jane remembered windows rattling and being knocked to the ground, even though Halifax was pretty far. Amos's belief was generally echoed in Demerett Bridge, making folks wary of the Germans of Raven River, second only in unpopularity to the Mi'kmaq of Indian Brook.

Mind your p's and q's, Rilla warned every time she

took her girls out to the insular community where she picked up washing for two men. Don't touch anything and don't stare were standing orders. Elva asked what to call them. No one had offered real names to Rilla and she wasn't asking. Not as long as they paid for their laundry, which they did. But they were some strange. The men weren't related, although Big Head treated Squirrel Boy like an imbecilic younger brother. Loud and lots of orders.

The only woman Elva knew to come into their lives, apart from Rilla scrubbing out their underpants, was a deeply lined, rail-thin ghoul who guarded the front porch and tried to keep the birds out of her potted begonias. Rilla said she was Mother Big Head or Mother Squirrel Boy, not sure which because they acted embarrassed by her and said nothing, but she was certain Mother Whoever wasn't right in the head. The old gal didn't speak English and spat at Elva as she sat waiting for Rilla, partially because Jane stuck her tongue out at her and made faces. Then one visit, the old dame in the even older clothes wasn't on the steps with her begonias and gardening tools and Rilla said she'd been sent back to Germany. Jane didn't believe it and on the way home in the truck told Elva she was murdered and buried in a trunk in the attic because she howled at the moon at night and kept everyone in Raven River awake. That's just talking loose, said Rilla. But, as Jane pointed out, at least the mosquitoes wouldn't bother her anymore.

But in the strange category, nothing compared to how the men lived. Why? No one knew. Jane hated to agree with Amos on any point but she conceded they must have been spies, hiding something, or from someone, to live in an immense wooden house built over sinking pilings driven into that bog. A makeshift plank bridge with rope guardrails was the only egress over ooze that rose during spring, and remained high through summer, setting the house in a moat, home to the fiercest mosquitoes and hungriest blackflies ever known. Elva always left swollen and itchy with bites and stings. They didn't seem to care for Jane's blood.

An unsound architectural vision and, somewhere along the way, the money running out left a legacy of turrets, gables, sagging balconies and arches rotting amid piles of timber, warped bundles of shingles, glass-empty window frames, rusting saws and trusses.

Elva had only been inside once. The entrance hall was dominated by a staircase to nowhere, guarded by a headless suit of rusting armour. Most of the second floor was uninhabitable, the few rooms reached by the ladder at the back of the house. Bare walls, rough railings, torn scaffolding and dust—dust thick like volcanic ash that threatened to bury the gilding of the ornate furnishings, oriental carpets and paintings of grey-skinned, black-eyed women with barely concealed breasts.

After that one time inside, from the way the two men stared at her daughters, Rilla thought it best to have Jane and Elva wait on the porch or in the Ford, where Elva coloured on old newspaper and Jane sighed to pass the time.

Nonetheless, the few coins Raven River brought Rilla were welcome during this long strike, and now that the supper dishes were done, she put water on the stove. There'd be double the cash in it for Rilla if she did overnight service, so there were hours yet of being up to her chafed elbows in steaming water and hauling sheets out by lamplight to dry in the dark. Elva, seeing how it was with her mother, offered to make tea. A quick cup and then on to the laundry.

"Where is he?"

Rilla never referred to Amos as her man or her husband. It was just *he*, or *him*. Not to make a point, mind you. Rilla wasn't like that. Too busy trying to hold it all together. With a wilful daughter in Jane and the likes of Amos, that meant, most often, stopping them from killing each other.

At least that wasn't a worry as far as Elva was concerned. She'd been born at Kirchoffer Place after Rilla and Jane took up with Amos. Such a baby, townies conceded, was a sign that God damned miscegenation—you know, the poison tree, poison fruit thing. Although Amos couldn't bring himself to strike his own flesh and blood, he sure didn't like to be reminded that Elva was his, so Rilla'd never ask Elva where her *father* was.

Elva said he'd gone to bed. Stomach ache. Again.

"Go ask Jane to get some milk and warm it up for him. I've only got two hands."

"I can do it."

"You'll spill it." She meant to add, With that arm of yours. It wasn't enough that Elva's knuckles were, by thirteen, hardening up into painful knobs, she had to be born shorn of any usefulness by a withered arm.

The kettle started to whistle. Elva ran her fingers over the back of a kitchen chair. When it was just the two of them, Rilla'd let Elva help. Go on then, make the tea, she said.

"Did it get fixed?" Elva asked, climbing on the chair to reach the tea tin.

"What?"

"The clock."

Rilla sighed and closed her eyes, thankful for the moment's rest. "Oh no, girl. By the time those boys were finished with him, he could barely stand up."

"Was he hurt much?"

"Some cuts." Careful, she added, watching Elva pour the hot water. "Didn't know Dom Barthélemy had a dog," she said by way of an afterthought.

It caught Elva off guard. She was about to say, He got one, too?

"And I think he knows that young fella trying to fix the clock."

In Rilla's telling, the bus to the city was loading so

there were lots of folks about when Dom found the boy sitting underneath the clock. They looked like they were happy and scared — both at the same time — to see each other.

Elva put out the tea things and slipped into the chair across the table from her mother. It felt very adult to her. So then what?

Rilla shrugged. Didn't notice. She had had the floor to finished scrubbing, hadn't she?

GIL HAD COME BACK and Elva refused to think about it, preferring to save the idea so she could savour it in bed, when Jane, beside her, was asleep. She had to concentrate on her dinner to do it, making fields of snow out of her potato and causing Amos to snarl, You want a slap there, girl! Rilla glanced at her daughter sharply, but Elva didn't care.

Gil has come back to me.

That's what she believed, although Jane would have pissed herself laughing if Elva said it. No matter. Didn't Elva know first hand Gil had tried to leave once before and had stayed because of her, or so she believed? It wasn't so hard for her to make believe that it had happened again.

Dom and Gil came from the hamlet of Chezzetcook Bay, a scattering of spindly wooden huts perched precariously on stilts over the restless tide, squatting on blue rocks topped with shocks of gold seaweed like turbaned old men easing arthritic bones into a vat of cold water. Contemporary map makers decreed it had been a place of fishermen since 1760 with the settling of Acadians hiding from the Expulsion. Rilla knew her people had been making seasonal camps by the bay long before there was a Dominion. No matter. According to the textbooks, history didn't start until a white man showed up with a flag and a priest.

The boys were put out to field, supplementing the family income as it were, as soon as they were able to walk, poverty being the dogged lot of the Barthélemys. They regularly took the road through Kirchoffer Place, tar ponds on one side, Jane and Elva's ungainly mansard-roofed house—wider at the top than at the bottom—on the other. When they rode together atop Old Mickey on their way to Demerett Bridge to sell firewood or fish from their father's catch, Gil was always first, but Dom held the reins from behind. Considering how physically similar they were, Gil and Dom were like an object and its mirror reflection rather than two halves of a whole.

Sometimes Jane and Elva would go with the boys into town, gallantly perched atop that aging roan while the boys hawked their offerings of fresh cod. Dom and Jane could chat forever about stuff. Gil'd just shake his head and say, Silly beggars, those two. Elva was the quiet one, the one noticing the stares they got from the townies. Even though Elva was just a child, she'd figured out pretty quickly that *half-breed* wasn't a term of endearment. Don't you take no mind, Elva, Gil'd say, trying to make like the folks looking at them were the ones to be laughed at, but Elva always did.

Finding out that Gil wanted to leave Demerett Bridge that first time, leave behind, as Elva felt, the entire world as she'd come to know, startled her. The day had been grey with winter and began with the sharpness of a single shot ringing through still-sleeping white hills.

The boys had been unusually absent for days, and even though Elva thought she overheard Dom tell Gil that it was bound to happen and Gil replied angrily, Shut the fuck up, the idea that something was wrong still came as a surprise. Shortly after the gunshot, Gil passed through Kirchoffer Place carrying only a cloth sack, over trails of fresh snow that by day's end, would be dull with soot from the foundry chimneys. No sleigh. No Old Mickey.

Elva was at her window, keeping quiet to not wake Jane, and was using her fingers to draw pictures on the frosted glass. Hey, she said, not knowing if it was Gil or Dom, and wouldn't until he spoke. She pulled on her coat and slipped down the stairs and out the front door.

"I'm heading south."

So it was Gil. His dirty face was streaked with new tears he quickly brushed away. Thrusting out his jaw, he almost pulled off looking stoic. If he lowered his voice he sounded unafraid and maybe just a bit older. Then it didn't sound so much like he was running away.

A rent in the distant sky spewed broken cloud and sun over the sea.

"Can I come?"

Overwhelmed that morning in his father's old boots, an oversized coat hanging loosely past his knees, Gil shook his head.

"I'm going to Halifax. Maybe one day, even Toronto."

A place with more people than Demerett Bridge was a concept too great for six-year-old Elva. The very notion of going somewhere as mythical as Toronto elevated the eleven-year-old Gil to manhood in her eyes.

"I'll get work, and some day I'll have a big house with a stable in the back. Just for horses." He looked back in the direction of his home. Just for horses, he reiterated.

"Please, let me come?"

"No. No one can."

Elva fell in stride and tried to keep pace.

"Why away?"

"Pappa wanted me to shoot Old Mickey and I couldn't. I just couldn't. He said I was a coward and can't stand the sight of me."

That horse was legendary in Demerett Bridge. He'd been rescued from a rocky bluff near Chezzetcook Bay by Gil's father after a steamer hit a sandbar. The horse survived the wreck and swam to nearby rocks accessible only by sea. When Alphonse finally managed to free the animal by tying it to his dory and pulling it into the water, it fought back so hard it almost drowned from exhaustion. The poor animal was so weak from hunger and shock that a bullet through the head was the humane thing. No one, especially Alphonse, could have reckoned on the persuasive powers of the Barthélemy brothers.

For weeks Gil and Dom nursed him, persevering beyond the hopes of the most stalwart of grown men, grudgingly winning the admiration of their hamlet and reclaiming the life of the horse. Old Mickey took his place in the household, and wherever Gil and Dom went, so too went the much-loved horse.

"He got the cough." Gil fought to blink the tears back. "Said Old Mickey was my horse, more so than Dom's because I spoke first to keep him. Said a man wouldn't let an animal suffer."

"Oh, Gil, you didn't—"

"How could I? I never would, Elva! Dom did it. He's a better shot. I guess I'm not much of a man."

The last word was whispered, torn between the loss of a beloved pet and falling short of a father's yardstick.

Elva knew there was only one thing to do. Running back to the house, she gathered her life into a Red Rose tea tin: three crayons, a broken mother-of-pearl clasp and a hanky Rilla gave her embroidered with Jane's initial. Armed against the cold with a scarf and extra mittens, she hurried back. Elva slipped her hand into Gil's, walking along in a winter silence, broken only by her occasional deep sigh, grieving for his loss. Kirchoffer Place was soon behind.

"You really can't walk it, Elva. It's too far for you."

Yes I can.

But she was struggling with the deepening drifts. Gil put her on his shoulders and continued through snow-buried fields. The stacks of the foundry appeared and disappeared and the path meandered upward into the fir-covered powdery hills surrounding Ostrea Lake. Elva sang, making up the words because she didn't like to know how a song ended, a chickadee's voice cutting clear across long frozen shadows, holding at bay the wind that was struggling to shriek against their reddened ears.

"It's not for Dom, the sea. He gets sick. I'm different. And I'm big for my age. I'll sail somewhere where it's always warm."

"Won't you miss them?"

"No one'll even know I'm gone. All they care about is Dom. Oh, I don't mind. He's smarter and Maman is sure he's called."

"Called by who?"

"God. She says God wants him to do His work. I dunno. Never heard Him, I guess. Ever wonder what God sounds like?"

"I know!"

"No, you don't. Maman says you can't hear God 'cause you're a mongrel bitch on account of your mom's an Indian with no wedding ring and Amos is a drunkard."

Elva'd have to ask Jane, when she was finished running away, what mongrel bitch and drunkard meant but she did know what God sounds like. The clasp was making a tinny banging noise in the tea box like an idea that had to get out.

It's like when the wind curls itself and makes that hollow-shell sound, when you can lick the salt from the ocean off your face, when oat grass rattles before snow comes and winter gales bend it to the ground. That's what God sounds like.

Gil was not to be convinced by a voice that did not speak with words or spoke to lesser beings like Elva.

They stopped by the tracing of a barn in stone, its wood long since rotted away. The sliver of sunlight over the sea was diminishing rapidly with the short day.

"It's getting late."

Elva said she was hungry and did he think they'd be in Halifax soon?

At first, Gil said nothing. His eyes were firmly fixed in the direction of home.

"I expect Dom'll bury Old Mickey behind the stall."

They huddled together out of the wind. Gil, being the son of a fisherman and thereby prepared for such an expedition, emptied his pockets. They feasted on salt-water taffy and root-cellar apples he'd secured for his flight to freedom.

"Say, it's really dark."

But Gil was somewhere else.

"I'm glad I'm a twin. Part of me gets to always be here."

Gil sure wasn't like other boys she knew. He was more, like, soft. Fancy nancy, Amos'd say.

"I'd never leave my mother and Jane." The last of the taffy was slowly easing down the back of Elva's throat. Oh yeah? That's exactly what she was doing.

"Hey, look." Gil stood.

Down the hill, towards the lake, a tiny orange light bouncing. Then another. Another. A dozen, maybe more.

"Can you hear that?"

Gee-ohm! Gee-ohm! No one called for Elva.

Although it was faint and far away, Elva could hear in the raw voice of Gil's mother that she'd been calling for some time. Neither Gil nor Elva could know until later that broken ice on the rivulet up behind Elva's house had fuelled the worst of parental fears.

"Serves them right. Let them look," said Gil.

It sure was getting cold. Gil wiped his nose on his coat sleeve and sat down. He tightened his arms about Elva, all of Demerett Bridge, the shimmering sea and the churning heavens beyond, resplendent at her feet.

Let her sister have Dom. How strong and comforting Gil's arms felt. Like they belonged there. Like she had the right to them. For once, she didn't want to be Jane. She said, I don't care if no one's looking for me. I'll go to Halifax with you. *Like you said, serves them right.*

But Gil wasn't listening. Lights flickered on the horizon and he wondered where that ship was going. Probably somewhere really far where things like letters, if you wrote them, took months, maybe years, to get delivered. Then the reader would be much older than the words when they were written. Something could have even happened to the reader by then, and he'd never know.

"If I'm not there to help with the firewood, Dom'll have to load it and sell it all by himself."

Wood is heavy, Elva conceded.

The voices looking for them were carried the other way, out to sea. Silence. Only the wind now. Elva relaxed into Gil's arms.

"Did you bring shoes?"

She shook her head, which was under his chin.

"What happens if your feet get wet?"

He had a point, even if he hadn't brought extras for himself, and she was getting sleepy. Maybe they'd done enough running away for one day.

"That's Rilla's Sunday dress."

Jane's glowing skin was beaded with moisture from her bath, making the dress cling in patches to her body. Curls of wet hair stuck to her cheek as she danced about, saying Hotcha! Hotcha! to the music in her head, much too delighted at the prospect of a funeral.

"She won't know unless some little mouse tells her." Rilla was up with the birds that Saturday morning to return the clean laundry to the boys of Raven River. "Want me to go naked and shake my titties in front of Dom and Gil's mother? It'll be your fault if I go to jail."

Elva didn't think Jeanine Barthélemy would be happy to see the likes of them naked or otherwise. Hard piece of biscuit, that one. Jane rolled her eyes and shimmied to Charleston, Charleston . . . da, da, ta-da, da da da . . .

"Help me with these buttons." Jane was pleased with what the mirror was doing.

"Amos will see it when we —"

"He's sick in the shitter again. I warmed him some milk. And you're not coming."

Jane hummed some more, twirling in front of her reflection. Although not a proper funeral, it nonetheless felt sacrilegious to Elva for Jane to be dolling up for it.

"What if he drips on Father Cértain? You know. With blood?"

"Jesus Christ, Elva! The things in that knobby head of yours."

Jesus Christ was Jane's latest rage because, as she announced with full solemnity in the privacy of the room she shared with Elva, God did not exist. So it was perfectly all right to use *Jesus Christ* like any ol' word without fear of eternal damnation. As yet, that bold sentiment copied from screen flapper Joan Crawford hadn't been echoed in front of Rilla. Elva knew what their mother'd have to say to that.

"Well, you won't get close enough to see." Jane turned her gaze out the window while brushing her waist-length shiny hair. "You can't expect people to look at cripples at a funeral. It's just hurtful when they feel bad enough. Plain church's different. Being thankful it's you and not them makes them put more money in the collection. Looks like there'll be fog."

"Gil's *my* friend."

Hadn't that been the arrangement? Two brothers, so alike, Jane couldn't possibly need or want to covet both. One for her, one for Elva. And Elva always assumed that Gil was her, well, friend, on account that he was the brother no one seemed to care about. More so after the *Meghan Rose*. Only problem was, Jane never agreed to split them. Jane never agreed to anything that wasn't completely in her favour.

"You're nothing but a field mouse to him."

She smiled condescendingly while Elva, sitting on the window seat, looked at the black pond across the road.

Like a festering old scab.

That tar pond was more accurately a meandering gallery of holes caulked with decades of effluent from the foundry. Nothing, unless you counted Jane and Elva, grew round it. Pools of rain formed on its surface, reflecting oily disembodied rainbows. Strong sea winds flung bits of it against the road. Rilla had long since given up trying to keep the front of the boarding house on Kirchoffer Place free from this windborne menace; she devoted her attentions to the patch garden behind the shed. But tar found its way even there. Flowers in the yard were rare, and if they did bloom, Amos didn't want them stinking up the house.

Jane hated the ponds. The smell sickened her and made her feel dirty in the summer heat, a reminder that the south side of town was reserved for factories, the dead, and them. A bogeyman place where old people with their brains rotted out stumbled into quicksand-like tar ponds. Amos said, It's a kindness to their families because they'd never get their wits back and who wants to change shit-filled diapers on some eighty-three-year-old man who spits gibberish like a baby.

Just how many tar babies do you think are down there? Jane once asked Elva, fascinated with the idea of corpses being preserved forever.

That was the sort of folksy myth that kept you up all night worrying about keeping birds out of the begonias seventy years down the road. Elva didn't know, didn't want to think about that. Sometimes, on a moonlit, cloudless night, the stars reflected their way across the black surface as if the sky and earth had traded places. The ponds were kind of peaceful then. As though even in their corruption they had a reason. Still, there were times when Elva would find Jane by their window staring at them like an adversary. That could only be because of Buttons.

Elva couldn't remember the dog. Mostly what she knew was cobbled together from what she pieced from Jane and from the wooden crate Jane kept hidden underneath her bed. Missing lettered slats, what remained had faded: *FL RIDA ORAN ES*. It was the one thing left of Buttons, the only tangible proof that Jane had a father and was therefore not, as Amos claimed, crapped into the street from the arse of a mule.

Oh yes, her real father used to buy her lots of fine things, and not just on birthdays! Jane swore she always had new dresses when her father was around, not like Amos, who made Rilla make do so that eventually everything went from her to Jane to Elva to the rag bag. Buttons had been one such gift to Jane when she and Rilla lived on Breton Street.

Jane wanted to remember it as the house on Breton Street, posh like. Understandable, considering the landlord went by *Madam* and calculated her rent from the number of men who visited the women tenants. It was a walk-up that froze in the winter and droned with horseflies in the summer, spit-through walls and so leaky it couldn't hold out a sun shower. Jane never knew the rooms could be let by the hour.

Buttons came in the orange crate from a mating that bred an off-white mongrel with brown paws and three black daubs down his chest. Jane adored him and carried him everywhere even when Buttons grew too big. He suffered the indignity with a fierce devotion. Along with Jane's temper, they were a force best not confronted.

He died in a coal mine was all Rilla ever said about Jane's father. Amos was more forthcoming.

"Died in a mine? My goddamn shitey ass! That girl's old man could have been any one of a hundred fuckers, black, white, red, Christ, who knows? It's not like your old lady was particular."

Nor could Rilla afford to be. With a girl to feed, Amos's attentions may not have been wanted, but the alternative for an aging whore, albeit not yet out of her twenties, with a kid, was starvation. Initially, their business dealings were perfunctory. Amos hated the crawling filth and lack of privacy in the flophouse, so he made the fuck quick, Jane holding Buttons, crouching behind a towel tacked from the rafters, listening while he grunted hurriedly through his satisfaction on top of her mother. More than that, he hated paying for what he believed a man should get for free.

Too bad about the kid, he'd say to Madam when he made his weekly contribution to her "building society," that Mi'kmaq woman Rilla was a looker. Yes, Jane was a fly in the ointment like they say, or was she? Maybe Madam wanted to move in some new, unencumbered tenant? And that's how Rilla's hard-earned talents were had for free, by shifting her and Jane by the tar ponds, away from the prying eyes of snooty churchgoers, no one saying, How come you don't marry that woman? (As if they would, Rilla not being white.) Room and board for mother and daughter in exchange for, well, you know, and a clean house.

Buttons earned his keep by ridding the cellar of rats, but it wasn't enough to win affection from a man like Amos. When Amos was sober, he was tolerable. When he drank, Rilla started to exhibit bruises reminiscent of the same type Amos's wife had. What kept them together was the illusion of free will: Amos could toss out Rilla anytime he wanted, and Rilla could leave when she pleased. When Elva came along, that changed. Getting rid of his whore and another man's child was one thing, but his own? Even a child like Elva? Amos was a top man at the foundry. He had a position. And men like him had to honour their bastards. That's just what you did. Overnight, Rilla and her girls were permanent, and the boozing, and bruising, worsened.

Jane had enough sense to keep Buttons away from her mother's man, but she was wilful, and it was only a question of when those wills would collide. After a Saturday night in town, Amos staggered back to his house on the other side of the ponds, waking Rilla to find her monthly curse had ruined her. Goddamn you! Okay then, there were other ways for a man to let off steam.

At the first of Rilla's cries, Buttons flew off Jane's bed and into the hall, barking and scratching at Rilla's door.

I told you to keep that dog out of the house, Amos muttered, Rilla saying: No Amos please Amos don't Amos, it's not the girl's fault.

He flung open their door.

Jane gathered up her dog and pulled him to safety. Buttons saw the fierceness from Amos as a threat and wormed free, catching Amos in the hand.

Who could remember in what order what happened next? Jane struck by Amos? Buttons viciously attacking his hand? Rilla trying to drag her daughter out of harm's way? Did it matter? No one would forget how it all ended.

Snapping and barking, Buttons went down the stairs firmly clutched by neck and tail. Should have done this a long time ago, Amos was saying as if it were a decision to clean out the back shed.

Jane was all flailing arms and legs and, No! no! no! Fighting against Rilla with a strength so uncommon in a child that Rilla fell against the stair railings, breathless, knocked helpless as Jane threw herself on Amos.

Jane would never forget, Rilla did nothing after that to save Buttons.

She and Amos knocked and butted their way out the front door, scratching gravel across the road to the tar ponds. Ah fuck, yelled Amos when the dog bit him again, and he heaved the dog into the air. Buttons, twisting and yelping, fell into the muck and, struggling, quickly sank up to his neck.

Damn you, you little bitch. Amos pulled the girl off him. You want him that much? Upending her, he doused her in the pond.

My hair! she screamed, pulling at his clothes.

Rilla, following out on the porch, was all, Amos! Amos, please!

Shut it, you little bitch, and down Jane went again, coughing and sputtering.

But she's just a little girl, her mother said quietly. Buttons barked helplessly from his grave.

When Jane's hair, her beautiful hair, was thick and clumpy from the tar, so ruined that Rilla would have to shave it off in the morning, Amos dragged her back across the road. He snapped off his belt and bolted Jane to the front porch.

"There you sit! Goddamned tar. I'll never get the stink off me." Then, "You leave her be," he snarled to Rilla, pushing past, "if you don't want her in next to it."

Rilla, knowing full well the truth of Amos's warning, did nothing as her man continued his rant, tossing around pots in the summer kitchen, looking for soap to clean up with.

If the intent was a quick end for the dog, it did not happen. Buttons howled pitifully under the stars, trapped at the neck. Jane worked herself into such a state that when she could no longer scream, no longer cry, she vomited dryly, refusing to allow Rilla to put her arms about her.

Around dawn, Gil and Dom's father happened by with his rifle on his way home from rabbit hunting. He knew Amos. Not much of a Christian. Didn't care for Amos's highfalutin ways when he was sober, his mean streak when in the jug. Alphonse saw Jane tied to the porch, Amos's whore sitting beside her.

He acknowledged Jane. She was mute, doubled over at the belt, trembling. The dog was too far out, panting, too gone to save. Only one thing left to do. The humane thing. He nodded. You couldn't tell between the shot and the sound that came from Jane.

Sure, she was all sweetness and light now, getting into

Rilla's dress, but Elva'd seen Jane when she thought no one was watching, stare at those ponds too, that peculiar empty look in her eyes. Real empty. Dead empty. Like something had been eaten away inside, maybe from all that tar. Whenever Elva saw that in Jane, she wondered if Mr. Barthélemy should have put her out of misery too.

Rilla was half right. It was Gil who knew the clock fixer. They were coming up together from the beach, striding through those distant fields towards the cemetery on that unusually mild spring day. Let me see, Jane said, joining Elva by the open window. He's taller than Gil, Elva noticed even though they were on the other side of the ponds. Well, if they were heading that way, Jane said she must be late and raced out of the room. Speed was the easiest way to lose Elva.

Rilla was somewhere between here and Raven River, and since the strike, there hadn't been any boarders, Amos not exactly the credit-extending kind. The screen door in the summer kitchen had banged, so Amos was back from the shitter, sprawled now in front of the parlour radio. He was dozing, wrapped in a blue cigarette haze, drifting off to white men pretending to be black, which Elva thought was foolish 'cause who'd want to be any colour but white, singing about mammies, which was just plain foolish.

"Wait for me!" Elva called as she hobbled into the road. The cemetery in the Eye of the monastery was not far but there was all that grass clogged with breaching dunes. It made for hard going.

"Can't you leave me alone even for a minute?" Jane yelled back at her, but when she saw that her sister was determined she slowed grudgingly to a trot. Elva didn't know why she was so fired up to hurry. Rilla didn't want them to go and Amos sure wouldn't like it if he found out, and Elva said so.

"If you're going to yabber, I'll run, I will."

So Elva kept quiet, tried to keep up with Jane and wondered what the clock fixer's name was.

The gate was already open. They'd have to cross through the cemetery proper to get to the strip of pauper's field against the pond. Once there, they hid behind a polished maroon obelisk to one of Demerett Bridge's founding fathers.

"Get back, they'll see you," said Jane, but Elva wasn't touching the tombstone 'cause she saw cobwebs. Spiders can nest under your skin if you get bitten in a graveyard and then one day they'll be so many they'll crawl out your nose. Everyone knows that, and then they'd have to call her Spider Elva.

"Don't be so stupid," said Jane.

Apart from John Ingram, the sexton who for a price would dig even a suicide's grave, they watched Dom and his mother, Jeanine, bury father and husband. But where's Gil, his dog, and that clock fixer?

The unnaturally short corpse was trucked to the

grave on the back of a squeaking cart. Dom and his mother resembled the long granite faces tucked underneath the eaves on the post office building, holding up the roof. John gingerly lowered the canvas package into the pit. Stiff, the dead man fit in nicely, but John had to avoid touching the head. Still dripping.

"You're green," Jane said.

It all went to remind Elva of that other grave, and it was just like that Jane to act like it didn't exist. Elva couldn't forget. She started wiggling her toes. That was Rilla's home remedy for a poor stomach, not having any money for drugstore physics. Guess if you were wiggling your toes, you weren't thinking about throwing up. Wasn't working for Elva.

Beyond the tombstones, past the grape-leaf bars of the gates, the fields of spring seagrass, the black pond and the sea were quickly disappearing. Its coming reminded Elva of something she did when a drawing wasn't right, blotting out the scene, like this fog did, with a blue-grey foam. It was moving fast, already cold on her face and the inside of her nose. Elva wondered what it would be like to start over. Really start over. God drawing you all fresh again, getting you right this time. She pulled her sweater about her tightly.

That other grave was down by the beach where the Kirchoffer Place road turns from slate to sand. It was a small one. Only big enough for a bird, a sandpiper. Elva's sandpiper. Murdered by Jane.

The sandpiper was near dead in the pitch-like ooze when Elva found it, its wings black with tar. So weak, its eyes glassy, beseeching Elva, the poor bird meekly allowed her to carry it to the summer kitchen. You'll be better in no time, she said, fashioning a hospital bed out of a cylinder of Quaker rolled oats by cutting it lengthways and layering it with scraps from Rilla's sewing basket.

For two days Elva ministered to her patient, swabbing its feathers as best she could, not even leaving it to sleep. When she was not gently rocking the rolled oats box, she was outside turning over rocks and digging for worms and grubs, not knowing if sandpipers ate them, but hoping to entice the poor thing to eat.

It was after one of these forays that she returned to find Jane with the lifeless bird. She had just wrung its neck and there had been enough tar left on the bird to stain her hands.

She carefully laid it back in the oats box.

But I was cleaning its feathers with spirits, look, brown with speckles, right there in my hand, it let me, trembling, watching me, trusting me. Rilla was so angry 'cause I got black on my dress, but I couldn't let it suffer.

Elva sobbed convulsively, her muddy hands red with cold, wriggling worms falling to the ground.

"It was suffering." Jane spoke softly and unusually sympathetically. "And so were you. It was right to let it go." Now that Jesus Christ had no value, that was as close to religious dogma as Jane got.

Even though Jane helped plan an elaborate funeral for the sandpiper, which they buried on the beach with a procession and Our Father, Elva came as close as she ever had to hating her.

The sexton waited expectantly after the last spade of dirt had been smoothed over Alphonse Barthélemy.

"Damn you, John Ingram." It was softly said by the widow, but a curse nonetheless.

"It's the Church who makes you pay." What did he care as long as someone did.

"Pay for unblessed ground? No words of comfort?" She couldn't stand to look at him, pitying her.

Dom pressed a few coins into the sexton's hand.

That's when Jane made her move, stepping out from behind the obelisk, like she wanted to say something to Dom and maybe to his ma. Then from out of nowhere came Gil's dog, barking, tail wagging, going right for her. Shush, go away! No! Jane fell back, but not before Dom and his mother turned and saw what looked like Jane and Elva playing with a dog.

"You?" Of all folks to see Jeanine Barthélemy in her hour of trial, that half-breed girl from the other side of the tar ponds? It was too, too much.

Jane slowly stepped forward, pushing Elva back from view, yet tightly holding her hand. I'm very sorry for your loss, was all she managed with a stiff and very unnatural curtsy.

Dom's mother was not a large woman, and seemed as bereft of sap as bleached driftwood. But she was a forceful one. She had held her family together during hardship and want and was stoically determined to force what was left of them through the scandal of this death and into the exalted heights of redemption she was sure Dom's calling would provide. Come hell or high water.

"Jane's come to pay respects." Dom's eyes shifted awkwardly from his mother to Jane.

Elva's tightly gripped hand was starting to hurt.

"Her respects? Jesus, Mary and Joseph, she's not here for that! I know about her kind, like her mother."

Elva closed her eyes and grit her teeth. She could just imagine what Jane'd have to say to that Barthélemy woman now, the fact she was Gil and Dom's mother be damned. But Jane said nothing. Just stood there and took it. Elva couldn't believe it. When she finally dared to look, there was Jane, looking confused, sheet white, like she had her wind knocked out.

That same look had come upon Jane once before. Years ago now, even before that time Dom got real mad about the butterfly. A silly thing really. In other folks, forgotten with time. But not by Elva. Yup. Dom was madder than hell over it, and Elva'd remember that most whenever there was talk about Dom and God.

No one intended to climb the tree. It just happened. Gil and Dom were up the limbs of the towering

dead elm, like monkeys, in a heartbeat. C'mon, Jane!
dared Gil.

The tree bordered the Barthélemy property, and the
boys had been forbidden to climb it as their neighbour
wasn't partial to having Frenchies on his land, or over
it, as the case may be. Said he'd shoot them like turkeys
if he caught them and no law in the land would fault
him for doing it. But you could see into Mr. Dorion's
upstairs windows from high up that tree, and Gil and
Dom were at the age when they thought seeing Mrs.
Dorion in her girdle would be sensational, without
understanding why.

Bet she can't climb it, Gil had taunted. Dom said,
Of course she can, even if she is just a girl. That was all
Jane needed to hear. Her shoes scuffing against the
bark, her clenched teeth holding back her breath, she
worked her way up from branch to branch, snaking
around the trunk. See, I told you I can do it! Good,
Jane, good!

Elva shielded her eyes from the sun. Oh, to be old
enough to climb trees! Then, *snap, kerr-ack!* Jane free-
falling without a word, the sound she made when she
parachuted into the wild rugosa that coiled up against
the fence would forever haunt Elva.

Gil and Dom were down that tree fast, like maybe
they'd fallen as well. She's dead and it's your fault, Dom
said. Elva remembered it as strange, seeing the brothers
fight, like watching yourself fight yourself. She didn't

know who to cheer for. Dom threw first, and Gil said, Hey, cut it out! His brother charged, but Gil was always the stronger of the two and hit back. Dom was not to be bested and surprised his brother with a slap to his face that instantly gave him a bloody nose and would later add a purple aura around his left eye. Gil went down. Dom stood over him, breathing hard, madder than anything.

Elva started to cry. Jane wasn't moving, but she did look grand framed in rugosa. It didn't even look like she was breathing. Dom knelt beside her, desperate to do something but afraid to even touch her hand. She was white, like she'd gotten into Rilla's flour box. Elva wailed that Jane was dead, but really she was only winded. By suppertime she'd be pink because Rilla had to paint Jane top to bottom in calamine lotion on account of the poison ivy in amongst the blooms.

"You knew he's back?" Jeanine's attentions were swept off Jane when Gil and a tall, pale young man, a shock of purple on the side of his face, stepped into the open.

Dom stared at his brother blankly. "No. I—No!"

The widow shook off Dom's arm. "I prayed to God never to see him again."

Gil looked at his feet, and there was Major. The dog was still dripping from a drink in the fountain. Jane was scrutinizing the other young man, who didn't seem to know what to do. Elva thought this would be a great time to turn into a butterfly and flutter away over the coming fog to her fields of grass.

"How can you share one face, one mother, and be so different? I've got one good . . . one good son left."

Dom took hold of his mother.

"God's granted me that."

"Let's go," the good son said.

"You stay away, girl," Jeanine hurled towards Jane.

Elva was pretty sure that Gil then said, Jane's just being kind, her coming here. Jane, when they talked about the funeral later at home, said it was Dom. Jane was certain of that. Dom, and not Gil, had stood up for her.

"The rest of you, skedaddle," John said as he packed up his tools.

That's when Jane knelt beside the freshly filled grave and did a very peculiar thing. From her pocket she retrieved a flattened bouquet of mayflowers and placed them gently.

Elva sensed Gil's friend standing very close to her. He made her nervous. That's the worst state for you to be in, Rilla always said of Elva. Makes your mouth run on without thinking.

"That's because Mr. Barthélemy killed her dog for her," Elva explained very lowly so only he'd hear, but of course, he'd not know anything about that.

Gil was beside Jane, staring at his hands. She got up without help, dusted off her knees.

"Fuck, it's been five years."

"What did you expect?"

"I dunno."

"Did you think she was going to say it's okay? Gil? You did, didn't you?"

"It wasn't my fault."

From the silence that followed, Elva assumed that Jane herself believed Gil had a part in the death of his father, but she was mistaken. Jane didn't care.

John chased them out then so he could lock the gates. Fog was blowing in quickly now, like smoke from farmers' frost fires set to keep warm fragile apple blossoms. It would be worse than walking home at night when at least the lights of Kirchoffer Place from across the tar ponds acted as beacons.

Outside the gates the clock fixer said, "Give your mother a few days, then try and talk to her again."

Everyone stopped, Jane and Elva waiting for someone to finally say who the hell this guy was.

Gil gestured. "This is just Oak."

"Hello, Just Oak," Jane said.

Elva wondered if the cut on his face hurt, but that was too familiar a question and they'd just met.

"It won't do any good," Gil said, oblivious to Oak's apparent awkwardness. "Maman'll never change."

Nothing newsworthy about the Barthélemys' religious convictions, as far as Jane and Elva were concerned. They were Catholics, like Rilla, although Rilla was a lot more quiet about her beliefs, probably on account of Amos not being partial to papist mumbo-jumbo.

Gil once told the girls about a Sunday school his mother had made him and Dom attend and a Grey Nun in a wimple who made him toss out the daisies and day lilies he'd picked for her because she said they had bugs. He hadn't cared for Sunday school after that. The nun's lesson that particular morning was about sin and souls, and she drew a large circle on the board. The class of boys fidgeted, wishing they were stoning the whale that had washed up on the beach overnight, as Sister filled her circle in with chalk.

When you tell a lie then a hole appears in your soul, the nun explained when at very long last she was done with the art portion of the lecture. She wiped a hole in the chalk, and the blackboard underneath stained her carefully coloured-in white soul. Only God's grace through confession and penance and Communion can make it pure again. And God help you if you die with any of those black holes still on your soul. Apparently souls with holes sink to hell rather than float up to heaven.

Jeanine Barthélemy concurred and threatened Gil, without much result, that he should be more like Dom or his back talking and wanderlust would send him to the bottom of Chezzetcook Bay, fish swimming through the great big holes in his soul. Eternity at the bottom of the sea.

Dom was the floater in the family. Everyone said so. Nothing was going to mark the purity of that boy's soul. Always by Father Cértain's side serving Mass, not like Gil, who'd skive off to muck out stalls for a few coppers, even dig that pit for Amos when Elva's father needed to move the shitter. Anything but go to church. Sure, he'd catch it from his father afterwards, but like he said to Dom, The whipping's over soon enough and I still got the money.

So when Jeanine started saying that Dom would be her offering back to God, her priest-in-the-family, her desperate way of winning back favour against the Barthélemy litany of woes, it was generally accepted by faithful Christians in town. And so far, so good. Dom was as true as any mother could hope for a son to be. He put out the texts at Sunday school and picked them up at the end of lessons. In winter, he hiked over frozen Ostrea Lake from Chezzetcook Bay to tend the church furnace so old ladies with blue hair didn't get matching faces and fingers at first Mass. Dom studied hard and worked even harder supporting the family after his father's accident.

For every inch of bad in that boy, Jeanine liked to say about Gil, his brother had a yard of the Blessed in him.

Gil was making light of strangling himself with an imaginary clerical collar, saying Dom was a mommie's boy, but no one could see much in the fog.

Elva wanted to know if anyone asked Dom if he wanted to be a priest. She thought she heard something like a chuckle from that Oak fellow. Jane said, Shut up.

The fog had thickly set, and the dull, monotonous horns in the harbour were resounding in sequence. Elva was shivering. No one was moving. Where to now? Major sniffed, running in and out of them on the hunt for moles.

"Hey, Jane, your old man still taking in boarders? Would he take me? And Oak here?"

In Jane's opinion, Amos would truck with Lucifer if he could cough up coin of the realm. "Sure," she said.

They went single file, real close because of the fog. Elva knew they were nearing the beach because as the surf washed over the round beach stones, it giggled as it crawled its way back to the sea. She wasn't too crazy about the tall grass tickling her ankles though. What if it was something else? When the talk amongst Jane and Gil trailed off, Elva began to sing something about Barbara Allen in a scarlet town and broken hearts and Sweet William who died 'cause she paid him no mind and briars and red, red roses. She sang partly because she couldn't see and she was nervous, partly because she was happy being amongst the others. But it had a lot of verses and Jane finally said, Shut up, Elva.

At first Elva heard only them walking through the beach grass. Then from Major, a low steady growl.

"What is it, boy?"

They must have been closer to the road than they thought, for a car sputtered and roared. Headlights cut through the fog. Oak, behind Elva, said, Listen, hearing what they all heard now, something heavy jumping quickly towards them through the field. Major barked. Jane screamed but it was cut short as though someone put a hand over her mouth.

"Run!"

Elva hit the ground, felled by a force from the side, dull and blunt. She struggled, but was pinned. She thought she heard a lightly accented nasal voice whisper, Just give you a love tap this time.

"Lay still." It was Oak trying to shield her. His silver watch was pressed close to her face.

She couldn't tell how many there were, only that it must be townies back for more because of the clock, or, from the muffled cries, what was happening to Gil and Jane, but Major had a hold of something and only let go with a silencing crack. Elva's protector was lifted away to sounds like stones against an overturned hollow hull.

"Don't you touch him! Don't you fucking touch him! Oak?" That was Gil shouting.

His friend never let out a sound. When the pummelling stopped, whoever was responsible tossed Oak into the sand and went as shadows toward the car.

ON THE RADIO DOWNSTAIRS: *Runnin' wild, lost control; Runnin' wild, mighty bold; feelin' gay, reckless too . . .*

"He's got a funny name," said Elva. "Here." She offered Gil a mug of steaming tea thick with cream and honey, but he was still too upset to touch it. Amos'd be mad if it was just going to waste.

Jane and Gil had carried Oak to the boarding

house, Elva bringing up the rear. Literally. The uncon-
scious boy was too heavy for just Gil and Jane, and
Elva did her best to prop up his middle during the
staircase manoeuvres. Thankfully, Amos was slurring
consonants when they carried him in. Feebly stirring
from his stupor in front of the radio, he was easily
appeased by, They can pay.

"Fuck 'im goddamned, take 'im upstairs, then."

Amos'd not trouble a soul until morning. By then
Rilla, not back yet from Raven River—probably off by
the side of the road somewhere waiting for the fog to
lift—would be home to deal with the shakes, the pounding head and all the good things that came after swimming inside a bottle.

The room they put Oak in was next to Jane and
Elva's. It used to belong to Gentien Rangeard, a welder
from Labrador City, but he'd moved on when the
foundry strike went from weeks to months and no end in
sight. I've a family back home that must eat, he explained
with a what-else-can-I-do shrug to Rilla, knowing she'd
be in the lurch, her roster of boarders dwindling.

Gentien had happened upon Elva drawing one
evening on the porch. Amos didn't like to see her waste
time on such foolishness. Jane, well, Jane just laughed
at anything she did, so Elva often hid her scratchings.
She was startled, struggling by the last bits of light with
cows and sleighs and a farmer with a can of milk, when
the welder caught her off guard.

Bien! Such majesty, Mademoiselle Elva! he said in that silly teasing way of his. She had no idea what *perspective* in her art was, but Elva knew something was askew when she saw it. The welder dismissed her concerns. She was tickled. Jane said their boarder was just being nice, but Gentien insisted Elva present him with three of her finest works. He then fashioned frames for them and decorated them with pine boughs before he mounted them on his wall, so that Elva's images appeared to peek out from the trees.

The boughs had long since dried out and fallen off, but the pictures were as Gentien hung them, where Oak would be able to see them when he awoke.

He'd been pretty banged up. Lots of cuts and, Gil thought, maybe even a broken rib or two, but how would he know? They bathed and wrapped Oak Egyptian-like, from the neck to the waist, another bandage across the side of his face. Jane then slipped out to the summer kitchen to wash the blood out of Oak's shirt, not sure, judging from the stain, if it was worth saving.

"You should have told him about the clock so he wouldn't have touched it when he was waiting for you."

"He wasn't waiting there, he follow—He wasn't waiting," Gil said, running his hands through his damp hair. "It's all my fault."

The mug of tea was weighing heavily on Elva. She tried to offer it again.

"You weren't even there when he tried to fix it."

"What? For Christ's sake, Elva, it has nothing to do with that fucking clock! Oh, here. Gimme that." He snatched the cup of tea from her crippled hand, spilling it. "Jesus, Elva."

Jane returned and said the boy's shirt was hanging outside to dry. She fixed a plate of bologna and cheese, some bread.

"You probably haven't eaten."

"Can I count on service like this for every meal?"

Jane wasn't about wearing her concern for all to see, nor would she take it being made light of. She sat the plate down angrily on the nightstand. Oak groaned.

"Starve, then!"

Elva took a piece of cheese and handed it to Gil's dog without anyone seeing.

Too tired to offer more, a weak smile from Gil had to serve as an apology. "Just joking," he said.

"You should be thinking about who did this."

"Don't care." Gil closed his eyes and stretched out on the bed alongside his friend.

"*He* will," Jane said with a nod to the injured one. "And whoever did this to your friend shouldn't get away—"

"I'll take care of it, Jane. Like Elva says, just boys in town getting worked up. And he's not . . ."

That was all he said. Major took up vigil on the floor by his sleeping master. Amos would never agree to dogs in the house, but that was a tomorrow issue.

"What are we going to do?" Elva asked as Jane shoo-shooed her out of the boys' room.

"Nothing. You heard him."

Elva wondered if they should talk to the constable in Demerett Bridge.

"Like he'd do anything," Jane said. "Go to bed."

All right, but that didn't stop Elva from thinking it was some odd, Gil trying real hard not to be concerned over whoever this Oak was.

Elva thought sleep would come easily, but it was hot upstairs even with the windows open and there were all those things going through her head. The abbreviated version of Mr. Barthélemy being sunk in a hole. Gil. Lying face down in the fog, the sound of footsteps coming up through the sand. The poor guy in the next room, lumpy as a sack of spuds. The longer she stared, the bigger the meandering cracks in the plaster overhead seemed.

It was a bed she shared with Jane, who often slept with her arms about Elva. She liked to feel Jane's breath upon her cheek, pert nipples stirring against her back, but that night Jane kicked fitfully, practically throwing Elva out of bed until Elva got up, sat by the open window and rested her head on the sill.

From there, clouds like cormorants' wings hurried wildly nowhere. The fog had passed, leaving a cool-kissing wake cradling Elva into a slumber, thankfully dreamless, for even in her dreams everyone but she had dazzling smiles and straight limbs.

The snapping of the screen door awoke her. Rilla was home, talking at Amos, who was still snoring on the sofa, the radio crackling voiceless. Rilla snapped it off. Elva listened dreamily to her mother's voice say the fog was too thick outside of Raven River and she had to stop and that she'd almost been sideswiped by a fancy yellow car. Rilla'd remember that colour.

Elva used to wonder why her mother would have these conversations with Amos passed out here or there until Jane told her that was the only time Rilla could have a regular-like-normal-folks conversation with him. Elva expected that by now, Rilla'd be putting a blanket over Amos before heading up to bed.

When she awoke to the soft click, the sound of a door quietly closing below, Elva figured she'd drifted off and that the fragments of Jane rustling into her clothes, Elva saying where are you going, Jane shushing her, were just dreams. It was still night. Elva was still by her window, but through sleepy eyes, it was no dream that leapt into the fields skirting the pond. Jane? Elva stood up. It really was Jane! What time was it?

Slipping out onto the landing, Elva saw that it was all dark downstairs. Gil and Oak's door was closed. Rilla's too. The dog gave out a quick growl at her creaking on the stairs. Outside, peepers were electrifying the fields with shrill calls.

Whatever mysterious force drew Jane on compelled Elva, though not as fearlessly as her sister. Jane was indomitable by nature and unable to move any direction but forward. Once Jane had fixed her mind upon a resolve, she pursued it as a duty with all the advantages inherent with beauty. Elva watched, that was her lot. Everything about Jane fascinated her. She was a light so bright Elva herself cast no shadow, only withered from its heat. Although it was madness to be out again when reason decreed the men who had attacked them might be lurking nearby, Elva pursued her sister, her body palsied by fear, her heart succumbing to its nature.

The moment when there is as yet no real light, just a lessening of the dark, made Jane's shadow a bouncing beacon as she reached the end of the slate road by the beach and headed in the direction of Demerett Bridge, past the monastery, cutting inland through fields towards Ostrea Lake with its ring of thick fir-covered hills. The tidal lake was also the home to Ipswich Abbey.

Elva didn't know if fabulous cities like Halifax lay claim to unique places that haunt them. She did know that Ipswich Abbey haunted her. Poised on a miniature island in the lake, it was not an abbey at all but a labour of love easily walked to at low tide. Even at high tide, the surrounding waters were only a few feet deep and easily forded.

Of its owner, John Solomon Purvis, little was

known. He was from away and had owned the island
for decades, spending only the temperate months in
Demerett Bridge while transforming the scrubby
island. In addition to indigenous plants, Purvis culti-
vated English seedlings. Over the years oaks, cypress,
Japanese maple, Dutch elm, poplars and apple trees
grew into lumbering shade-bearing giants that looked
as if they might sink the small island, while beds of
colour clogged meandering walkways of blue oat grass.

When the century was very young and in the year
before the hurricane, the newly launched schooner
Meghan Rose sailed into Demerett Bridge, its hold brim-
ming with a special cargo for the island — stones from an
ancient kirk somewhere in Scotland that had been
demolished. The townies laughed over the expense of
such a folly. Sending rocks to Canada! Why it's like
shippin' coal to Cape Breton! Rumour was, even the
altar with the finger joint of some dead saint embedded
in it was included. The bits of old church were trans-
formed into garden art, a medieval wonder of turrets —
nested by the Ipswich sparrow, which gave the Abbey
its name — cloisters, roofless halls and arching bridges
over a shimmering pool.

It's for the woman he loved, Elva once made up to
Jane. "And from the top of the castle, you can see the
name Lenore spelled out in apple trees, so beautiful in
spring. No one knows who belongs to the name. She
had very pale skin."

Everyone was white in Elva's stories.

Through the screens of the summer kitchen, Jane and Elva could see Rilla enveloped by sheets on the lines, brushing the hair back from her face, adding more pins, getting eaten alive by squares of white.

"She died of a broken heart."

Jane preferred stories about jazz and necking parties and taking baths in tubs full of gin. No way flappers with lapis lazuli hair-bands would ever die of anything, let alone something so stupid.

"Must be from Cape Sable, then. The crazy ones come from there."

Elva thought about it. "From a town called Skyler."

"Never heard of it."

"Because it's gone now. Washed away in a hurricane. And that's how Lenore's real love perished." As in all the great romances, Elva knew, no one died. They perished. Wasting away coming a close second.

The screen door banged shut behind Rilla as she came in with her empty laundry basket, noting that potatoes won't peel themselves.

"I'm going as fast as I can do you want me to cut off my fingers and have bloody mash potatoes?"

"They'd only be pink potatoes," Elva said. She had put down her pencils and was shucking peas, so had nothing to worry about.

Don't say bloody, Rilla said on her way to get more wet sheets. She glanced at the clock. Big, round, with

Roman numerals. Couldn't help notice how much time until, or how much time left. Elva was to get that drawing stuff of hers put away before Amos got home and saw it.

"Mr. Purvis was in love with Lenore's mother but she ran off with a sailor."

"I'd pick the sailor too."

"So Mr. Purvis follows her to —"

"Montreal."

"Okay, Montreal, but she's had a baby and is dying."

"Where's the sailor?"

"Oh, he's long gone."

Figures. Wouldn't happen in a story with gin-soaked Shebas with bobbed hair.

"So he brings them back to Skyler where he builds a castle on a cliff and calls it Ipswich Abbey. It's like a prison and that's where he keeps Lenore because she looks so much like her mother that Mr. Purvis vows she'll grow up to love him."

In addition to everyone in Elva's stories being white and of course beautiful, they were always vowing something or other, then regretting it.

"In the basement he builds a room all out of marble with candles for the mother 'cause he's still in love with her too and remembers that she's afraid of the dark. He goes down there to talk to her."

"But she's dead."

"I know."

"You can't talk to dead people."

Jane was missing the point. "How do you think of those things? Is he rich?"

"Well, he builds ships."

"Then he's rich."

Rilla wanted to know what they were on about.

"Nothing."

"Nothing."

Rilla hated when her girls said nothing over something.

"Elva's making up stories about Mr. Purvis."

Don't you be gossiping, Rilla said, because in her books Mr. Purvis was a fine gentleman by all accounts. Never gave her any cause. The screen door slammed, punctuated with a Peel, girl!

"Well, go on."

Elva wasn't sure she would after that. Rilla was back at the lines stringing more sheets. Cripes, but laundry day went on forever.

"When Lenore grows up, she meets David from the town and falls divinely in love with him."

"You said Mr. Purvis kept her locked up. How could she meet someone?"

"I don't know everything!"

"It's your story, stupid. Well, go on."

They saw a sheet get away from Rilla. She'd have to wash it again.

Jane still had the same potato in her hand. There! there! there! She stabbed it with her paring knife. "I hate peeling potatoes. It's not fair you get the cripply arm and I have to do all the peeling. And you shouldn't say mister. Just call him Purvis."

"So they love each other so much that being kept apart makes them crazy and Mr. Purvis—and Purvis says, You'll have to marry me Lenore because you'll have no money without me and I love you and your mother in the basement said so. David can't stand to be away from Lenore so he runs away and joins the navy. Here she comes."

The screen door banged behind Rilla with the errant sheet. She went to the pump and rinsed it.

"But he can't stay away from Lenore," whispered Elva, shucking more rapidly. "So he comes back to her on a ship he stole but a hurricane's washed away the lighthouse even though Lenore went out there every night with a lantern to warn him. Just in case."

The ridiculous story didn't make any sense, but Jane had to know what happened next. Rilla was still making water at the squeaky pump.

"The ship hits the cliff in the dark and Ipswich Abbey crumbles down on top of it, sinking it, and David and Lenore are finally together in a watery grave."

What are you two whispering about? Rilla wanted to know.

"It's Elva. She thinks Purvis—Mr. Purvis—has a dungeon at the Abbey where he keeps dead ladies."

"I do not! I just made it up!"

Rilla said Amos would be back shortly and Mr. Purvis was from Connecticut who minded his own business so enough of that loose talk.

"How come I have to do the peeling and Elva doesn't have to do anything?"

Their mother said Elva was doing her share, but it sounded as if she meant, Be thankful, girl, you're not like her.

"Fine. Not my fault if we have pink potatoes."

At the shore of the lake, Jane tied her skirts around her waist, waded through the shallow water, her shoes held overhead, and vanished from Elva's view.

Why come here? No one comes here. Anything could happen and no one'd ever know! Jane!

The last thread of her courage snapped. Elva could bear no more, go no farther. Running as best she could along the beach after her sister had been one thing, but once Jane dashed across the road and into the fields towards the lake, Elva'd gone too far, and knew it. Scared: plain and simple. No telling now if the dull clanging was the distant channel marker bobbing in the swelling tide or Elva's racing heart. Farther ahead were twinkling orbs of yellow and orange circles: lights from Demerett Bridge. Here was darkness and shadow. Behind, nothing but that occasional yawn of the surf preceding the thunder of sea on sand and splashing foam.

A thin line of azure appeared on the horizon in that place that spawned fog. As angry as she knew Jane would be, Elva had to find her sister and plead with her to take her home. That meant crossing into the lake and the tide was in. Muddled, Elva forgot to remove her shoes. Now they were wet and Amos would be furious if he saw them ruined.

Hello Mary!

It felt more right to Elva to start the prayer off that way. Hail sounded like Gil and Dom when they used to pretend to be Roman soldiers. Rilla always said to pray to the Virgin when you were in trouble, but now Hello Mary full of grace wasn't working. Nothing was working. Her breath began to clutch, a prelude to tears, when she noticed a faint light in the Abbey's faux cloisters.

"I was afraid you wouldn't come."

Even whispered night voices could be heard from a distance across the lake, so Elva, much relieved, knew Dom was with Jane as she crawled up on the shores of the island and wrung out the folds of her dress. Through the Abbey's wispy birches rose the arches of the roofless cloister under a cavernous oak, the breeze jostling its dewy leaves. They were inside. Surrounding the rows of columns, white rhododendron, gone grey in the infant morn, along with Elva. Watching.

"Someone followed us home." Jane covered Dom's face with kisses. "I had to make sure they were gone. And my mother was late getting home."

Dom grabbed Jane's face in his hands. "Are you okay?"

A kiss for a reply.

"Was anyone hurt?"

"They went after your brother's friend."

"Why?"

"I dunno. Something he did to the clock in town, I think."

"You shouldn't have come, Jane. It's too dangerous."

"Fine. I'll go."

"No! Don't." This time, Dom kissed her.

"Did you really not know he was back?"

"No. But he's not here to honour our father. I know that much."

"No forgiveness for the *Meghan Rose?*"

"I would if he'd admit to what he did, but Gil's a coward. He ran away. Can only imagine what he's done that he has to come back now."

"Never thought I'd see him again. No one did. Except Elva."

"Why did our little Miss Elva think that?"

"Shut up about her," Jane said, gently biting as she struggled with his shirt.

His chest, matted with dark hair, flinched under Jane's teasing tongue. Dom pressed Jane to him as he pulled her to the ground, wrapping his arms about her.

"What is it?" For Dom was aware that Jane had gone still, momentarily eluding him.

"I see your mother's face, Father Domenique. What would she say if she could see us now?"

"Don't mock my faith."

Jane'd accepted being second to God because that meant nothing to her, but be damned, she'd not come after his mother.

"Tell her, Dom. Tell her soon."

Elva was not ignorant of what happens between men and women, nor had there ever been any mystery or wonder surrounding it. Jane, growing up in the house on Breton Street, had regaled Elva with mechanical details. Never pretty; dirty, sweaty, hardly romantic. Then there was Rilla and Amos during their Saturday-night ritual, Elva not quite sure if their noisy coupling was giving them pleasure or pain. But this, what happened before her now, this was something else. Not the fumbling of a teenage boy and his girl. Not a friendship blossoming into more. How could Elva have missed noticing two natures whose essential elements required the other until, simply, this fusion?

Elva lay under a flutter of rhododendron blossoms like one starved, feasting upon someone else being loved, certain that she was somehow sinning in the watching, not them in the doing, and unable, unwilling to turn away. No longer enough, wanting to be Jane.

Elva awoke with a start.

What about the white rain and running her fingers over the tidal ridges of beach sand as he held her? No, that was his chest against her face. Someone had carried her. He carried her. *His hands, hard, they were hot.* Elva remembered asking, What about Jane? And he said, What about you, my little marionette? I came to get you. Don't you love me? *Yes!* Like a blanket he covered her, a snail traversing her neck, leaving sticky brands that tingled in the cool, sweet air of morning. She breathed his breath. *He rushed into me!* Then he looked sad and asked, Why did you have to be ugly?

"What's the matter with you? You sick?" Jane said, hastily scrubbing her face with water from the pitcher on their bedside bureau, shuddering from the coldness of it.

No, the same. Elva shook her head. Only a dream and they have a way of becoming nightmares by day.

"You'd better hurry. Rilla's ready for church."

Lingering in bed, Elva tried to clear the still powerful images from her head, voices that whispered from across the night.

But Jane?

And he'd said, not to worry, she's coming. Go to sleep. It's better if you sleep, before she gets back. Say nothing. Say nothing, Miss Elva.

There was an anxiousness in her abdomen she had never known before. Confusion. She sat up. That face in the mirror on the bureau grinning back at her, but not happy, wobbling, saying, See, I *am* a goblin.

"Did you sleep in your dress?"

Elva looked. She had, and stiffly got out of bed.

"Jesus!" Jane had her hand over her mouth. "Look, you're a woman now!"

Oh! And Elva noticed the blood too.

Jane was laughing, Rilla! Rilla! Leaving Elva to mark her womanhood by hiding her shoes, with their saltwater stains, under the bed.

OAK'D BEEN PROPPED UP by his window watching
Elva hunched over on a log by the end of the driveway, drawing.

"Hey! Gil says you painted these pictures up here.
That fisherman and the sleigh and those cows in the field,
I pretend they're pieces of a story. I really like the black-
and-white cat with the red smile. Helps me pass the time."

Elva ignored him, expecting ridicule to follow.

"I like them!"

"Hey, back," she'd said, looking up.

The bruising had set in. Oak sounded awful.

"Thanks for last night, you know, getting me back with the others."

Elva asked how he was feeling. He was sure he'd broken a few ribs, but all things considered, he'd be okay.

"You some kind of a doctor?"

No, he replied, but he'd had broken ribs before and knew what to expect. Oak didn't elaborate.

"Whatcha doing?"

She could have said, Trying to keep my head from spinning off or worms eating through my heart or my skin from moulting. And she was angry to boot! Boy, was she angry, with a whole new sympathy for poor ol' Eve of Eden, who just happened to be fodder for Father Cértain's Sunday sermon that morning. But the priest had it wrong. You didn't choose to eat from no damned apple tree, it just happened. Then God made you pay for not having any choice at all! Like Elva's trip to the Abbey, which was still a muddle of half-truths and what-was-real and why did Gil keep popping up in the middle of it all, a dream in which he carried Elva home? She didn't want to see that Jane was changing from the beloved image of a bare-footed sister, arms caked with sand when she and Elva dug for clams, into something that would take her away. But when Dom fucked her—and that's how Elva thought about it, that's the word she used because she didn't want to think anything nice about him changing Jane, and she thought it with the same intensity as *I hate you*—so when Dom fucked Jane, Elva understood from it that Jane would know life, she'd know want. Haw haw, said God.

But Oak was just being polite when he asked, Whatcha doing? So Elva scribbled harder and faster and said, Nothing.

Amos let Rilla have it when he realized she'd agreed to Gil Barthélemy staying with them. As good as a murderer, he said, at the very least a coward, which, because Amos's illness did not affect his voice, worked up to a goddamned-Jesus-fuckin'-Christ roar when he was in the jug trying to drown out the pain in his gut. Then it was best to keep doors shut, your head down, until his drink du jour, usually bourbon, worked its magic.

Rilla didn't care. She was thankful to have Gil and his friend as paying boarders even if Oak didn't take kindly to her nursing at first.

"Why do you think?" Elva asked, carrying fresh bandages for her mother.

"You have to relearn some folks that not everyone wants to hurt them."

"Who did that?"

Rilla didn't say.

After Oak first asked Elva to show him her sketch book, she shyly began to sit with him and Gil when she drew. The silence was unnerving. Elva sure didn't remember Gil being bereft of the gift of gab, simultaneously skittish to be elsewhere and obsessively worried about Oak. For her part, Elva was still trying to understand why she felt like she was going to jump out of her skin. She hadn't yet even begun to get her head around what people would say if they found out about Jane and Dom.

"Well, then, read to me if you both won't talk," Oak said.

On the nightstand was a copy of *The Great Gatsby*. Rilla kept it as a decoration. No one had read it, nor could she remember where it came from. Rilla said one of the factory workers must have left it, and judging from that lot, it had to be dirty. At least naughty. She didn't think it proper to listen to Fitzgerald's tale about men in love with other men's wives.

Jane, who flirted with the idea of changing her name to Daisy, or at least Daisy-Jane, was enthralled by Gil's theatrical delivery. He made her laugh and Jane liked to laugh.

"Who am I?"

"Yes, who's Gil," said Elva as Jane assigned characters to all.

Gil would have to be Daisy's husband, Tom, but of

course, Daisy was really in love with Gatsby. No one had to ask who Gatsby was.

And Oak? He'd be Wilson the mechanic. Probably on account of the clock business. Rilla could be Miss Baker, although no one could picture her lounging around, playing tennis now and then.

"What about me?" said Elva.

"Yes, what about Elva! Elva needs a role!"

She could be the creepy eyes on the billboard.

"But that's not a real person!"

From downstairs, Amos banged the wall. Guess he must have overheard Gil because he said shut the fuck up about those rich Jews up there. Amos figured all wealthy Americans were Jewish.

The readings progressed much more quietly over the next few days, the perfect balm for the ache of reality, but somewhere betwixt East Egg and West Egg and Wilson getting it wrong, shooting Gatsby in the pool, the eyes of Dr. T. J. Eckleburg watched Jane watching Gil.

Put up a roadblock and it was bound to happen to one as emotionally hot-wired as Jane. Jeanine Barthélemy wouldn't stop short of having Jane burned as a witch if she knew where her saintly son had been, and Rilla, well, Rilla would know all too well how tenuous their situation with Amos was. Any scandal and he'd dump them like garbage. Add to the mix the danger of so many idle men lollygagging around town, especially after what had happened to Oak, and there was no way Jane could slip out alone any more to be with Dom.

But she could pretend she was with him, and Elva knew it.

Can't they see, him acting out when that Gatsby speaks 'cause Jane likes it, watching her over the top of that book, her sittin' there all queenie-like, and I know she's pretending he's Dom.

Jane's glances lingering too long, sitting too close. As Elva knew and feared, it brought Gil pleasure when it wasn't meant to. When she realized it too, Jane flashed him that haughty look of indignation, turning away angrily as much to chastise herself for being unfaithful to Dom as to distance Gil. But the pained expression was on a face like Dom's, and if being angry with Dom was impossible for Jane, Elva wondered, how come no one sees?

Elva was wrong. Someone else did see, felt what Elva felt and worried that Gil was falling in love with Jane.

Moths bumped against the screens in the warm evening air. The kitchen calendar had a new month and a new advertisement: Ipswich Baking Powder. Elva refused to look at it any more. She was boycotting it. The name reminded her of what was trouble waiting to happen and she'd rather forget. Amos continued speculating without anyone paying too much attention.

"There's something not right about that friend of Barthélemy's," he said, Oak being more noticeable now that he was up and around. "He doesn't speak much."

Jane was at the stove, stirring some milk Rilla asked her to watch. Her back was to them like she was trying to blend in with the cupboards.

"And what's the matter with you these days, girl?" he asked Elva, who was helping Rilla clear the table. "You're too damned quiet as well. Gives me the creeps, you sitting around all day. What are you always drawing, anyway?"

Elva tried to carry too much with her weak arm and the dishes clattered back onto the table, knocking the salt shaker onto Amos's lap.

He jumped up and pushed her away from the table, then threw salt over his shoulder.

"For Christ's sake, can't you do anything without making a mess? As if I didn't have enough fucking bad luck with the lot of you."

"Those boys pay their board." Rilla skilfully gathered up the plates and deflected Amos's anger away from Elva.

"Yeah? How, is what I'd like to know. Where's Barthélemy getting the money?" Amos said, his eyes blazing on Elva as he sat back down.

"All I know is that they're out early and not back till late," Rilla said, the tablecloth straightened. "Must have work somewhere."

"In this town? Who'd hire Gil Barthélemy?" Holding his stomach, he added, "Fuck me, woman, if you aren't becoming the worst cook in Demerett Bridge."

A dollar a week, Gil offered next evening after he and Oak had returned.

His hand was on Elva's shoulder during the asking. She was cataloguing in her mind all the physical occurrences between them. This time his hand was heavy and warm with an oh so gentle squeeze. *Does it feel the same as Dom's? Would Gil touch Jane like his brother? What would it be like if Gil touched me that way?* And Elva turned her blush away.

It was a princely sum to look after a dog. She took the job as offered not for the money but because Major had taken readily to her. The only warm-blooded thing to ever kiss her. (No, that wasn't entirely true. That mousy Harry Winters had been dared by his older brother. There was a penny in the doing, but he cried after and said he'd got warts. Rilla? Well she had to, so that didn't count.) So Major was the only warm-blooded thing to ever *want* to kiss her, and he didn't care if Elva wasn't straight limbed or creamy skinned. Making sure he was fed and watered was something she'd have freely done. Even so, the money heightened Elva's curiosity. Where *was* it coming from?

Solving the mystery wasn't planned. It just happened, a sort of what-if-I'm-out-and-see-where-they're-going kind of thing, Elva rationalized early next morning when she was taking Major for his walk. It surprised her when the boys headed not in the direction of town but in the opposite way until Gil and Oak were nothing more than specks on the Old Narrows Road.

The sun was washing steadily over green hills, splashing down into Demerett Bridge. Not a rainy May this year. The flat roadway ahead afforded Elva an easy view as she sauntered along, Major sniffing at grass roots, Elva trying not to look just in case the boys turned and caught her. When they stopped to sit by the side of the road, stripping off their shirts against the heat, Elva led Major into the tall grass and said, Quiet now.

The dust cloud on the road beyond Gil and Oak moved quickly, stopping suddenly, a bus swallowing them whole. Then it turned off the Old Narrows Road and swaggered onto a long-unused carriage lane that once skirted all the way around Ostrea Lake. It made its way to the back entrance of the steelworks, slipping into the compound of the Maritime Foundry Corporation through the myriad of plywood sheds, chimney stacks and roofless outbuildings dotting the scarred land behind the main complex. The cloud vanished and Elva could follow no more.

So Gil and Oak were scabs. Hadn't Amos been saying that all along, and while he had no love for the company that turned him loose as soon as he was too sick to work, well, scabbing was unforgivable. A man just didn't do that kind of thing. Sure, Elva wasn't a hundred per cent certain why scabbing in a labour dispute was so wrong, but she figured by the way Amos went on about it that Gil and Oak wouldn't want him to find out and her old man wouldn't want to know. The day still ahead, Elva scratched Major behind the ear and said, C'mon, boy. There was her hideout to see.

A small door in Elva's closet led to a cramped space, several feet high, running the length of the house under the skirting of the sloping mansard roof. Amos's wife, Dotsie, had probably had plans to use the space for storage, but other than an ancient hornet's nest, the crawl space had never been used.

It had become a sanctuary of sorts, like when Amos got really sauced, knocking Rilla about, shoving his gun in her mouth and saying, Shut it you cunt or I'll blow your fuckin' head off and them little cunts upstairs too. The girls would crawl inside, sometimes crying themselves to sleep in each other's arms while Amos raged down below.

After Buttons died, Jane didn't use it much. She was getting too big to get through the door, and Elva noticed her sister more prone to stand up to Amos than hide from him. Like that time when he said she paid too much mind to her hair and she said so what and Amos dragged her out onto the porch and wanted to cut it off. But he didn't.

So the crawl space became Elva's place and she used it not just to hide from Amos but when life in gen-

eral felt like too many voices speaking at once. It was
hot in the summer, draughty in winter, lit by lines of
light from a vent at each end, stained with watermarks
from the leaking roof. Here Elva would curl up on ratty
horse blankets, overhearing the men her mother let
rooms to go on about poor wages and Rilla's breaded
pork chops and Jane's tits, Rilla singing in the kitchen
about sweet chariots that would come and take her
home, Amos yelling across the backyard from his shed
to shut the fuck up, while Elva drew, papering the cedar
planks with her secret voice.

One more thing. From all that time spent colouring,
Elva knew from a crack in the plaster that she could
hear everything plainly, and provided the closet door
was open, she had a clear view of the room next to hers.
Gil and Oak's.

"I expected it today. There isn't a window on that
bus that ain't broken," Gil was saying that evening, sitting at a table, adding what looked like sums in a ledger.
"The union's soon gonna figure out how the foundry's
getting us in."

Oak was sitting on the bed, tools arrayed in front of
him, a watch in pieces in his hand. He was having a
hard go with his tinkering.

"I wish we didn't have to work there."

"Money's good."

"We're not suited to this kind of work. I ache all
over and my hands are cut up."

Gil snapped down his pencil. "I didn't ask you to follow me! I'd be gone now if it weren't for you getting the shit kicked out o' you."

Oak leaned back against the headboard.

There was silence for a while, then Gil hung his head over the back of his chair.

"I need this job, Oak." It sounded apologetic.

"If we squared things with Bryant — "

"I was dead the minute I ran, we ran. You know that." Gil turned back to his ledger, like maybe staring at the figures long enough would magically come up with more money. "I said I'll get us out of here and I will. Schooners are running rum along the coast all the time. We'll get to Florida like I said. Maybe Mexico. We just need a bit more money."

"What if we get caught? I heard Americans shoot bootleggers and dump them overboard so they don't waste time with jail."

"Stay here, then, and take your chances from the boys in Halifax. You know what that beating you took was really about."

Below the ceiling, Amos's snoring said he was dead for the night. Overhead, the ping of rain on the shingles. Elva was about to crawl back to her room when she saw Oak put away his watch hobby, get up, hesitate, and walk over to his friend hunched over his calculations.

"You're tired," he whispered, his mouth close to Gil's ear.

Gil shrugged him off. Oak persisted.

What's he saying? Louder! Elva pushed her ear against the crack in the plaster.

Then Oak pulled a resisting Gil to his feet and wrapped his arms about him.

"No—"

The sound of Gil's voice was cut off by Oak's embrace, his lips pressed to another man's.

"Come to the bed."

They kissed like they meant it, Gil then offering half-hearted resistance and a feeble, No. Oak pulled back, as if this demonstration of virtue was some sort of ritual that had to be played out. Gil came back angrily. There'd be nothing tender in this, peeling off vests and shirts, the pale shades of their skin soon caught up in the sheets, little boys running, laughing, playing in the surf like a day at the beach. Elva, wide-eyed, remembered what Jane said about Gil having an undertow.

She pressed closer to see, at risk of breaking through the wall, shaking, no context, unable to turn away. Even Jane had not whispered this touching between men to her. Part need to master, part desire to succumb, their wrestling for release left them wet and satiated and panting hungrily for air. When they were done, Elva brushed away the wet from her eyes. Not because they were beautiful. Not because it had been beautiful. But because Gil was supposed to be hers. *Mine!* And Elva bit into the horse blanket.

"Not again. Not here. It's not right." Gil clung to the edge of the bed. He hadn't said: never again. "Jesus, I hate you for this."

"No, you'll never hate me."

Gil rubbed his hands through the hair on his chest and down his belly as if his hard body was both a joy and a curse to his touch.

"Do you think your brother will become a priest?"

"Why?"

"I know you."

Gil smiled. "I didn't tell you this. The night you got whacked, I followed Jane out to the lake. My brother was waiting for her. I haven't been out there in years. Even in the dark, it's wonderful, still wonderful. Perfect place to go if you don't want to be found. I was just a kid my first time there. I'd seen those towers from the shore, but never up close. Maman forbid it, something about that man who built them made her people pack up and leave Grand Pré a million years ago, but she blamed that on anyone who spoke English. So I stole a canoe and rode out from the other side of the lake. No one saw." He chuckled.

"Old Purvis had seen me coming and greeted me like I was the King of Siam. Walked me through his gardens, pointing out every tree and flower in Latin, like I knew what that was. Odd sort of fellow. Still is, I guess."

Oak was not paying attention. Why do you look at her, why do you try and be around her, why do you need to please her, what do you want her to see in you, why, why, why? But all he said was, "Why'd you follow her?"

"I dunno."

"They're lovers, aren't they?"

"Well, Dom fucked her."

"You surprised?"

"That she's like an animal? Partly, I guess."

"And that he's a . . . man?" Would Oak have said, Normal?

"How could I be half my brother and not know that side of him?"

"He doesn't know this side of you." Oak caressed his friend's back. Gil said, Don't.

"How long do you think they've been that way?"

"Jealous of your own brother?"

Oak had Gil's arm and tried to pull him back, but Elva was no longer paying attention.

Gil *had* been at the Abbey! He must have brought Elva home. *I was in his arms!* She hadn't lost Gil to Oak. She was sharing him!

She lay back, hugging that sweetness to herself, smiling at the wooden slats overhead.

The popping of glass and a barking Major woke Elva and Jane and they rushed to join Gil and Oak on the landing. Below, Amos was picking up the stone hurled through the front-door window.

"Pink-whiskered Christ!" Amos looked from SCAB, crudely painted in red on the rock in his hand to Gil and Oak. "You bastards! I heard wind the company was . . . I knew you were up to something, Barthélemy!" The aggravation was churning up his stomach. "Did you know about this, bitch?"

Rilla shook her head.

"They're out by morning, or by Christ—"

Gil and Oak denied nothing. "We'll cause you no more trouble, Mr. Stearns."

Elva felt Gil's hand lightly graze her back, and flinched the flinch of the guilty. There'd been no looking him or Oak in the eye, convinced she'd find, we know about you watching us.

Couldn't they stay? Elva wondered to Jane as she crawled back into bed. Her sister didn't seem to care. Jane sighed the kind of sigh that wanted Elva to ask, What's wrong? But Elva didn't. She had her own things bumping around inside her head that needed working out. Jane was on her own.

From downstairs, the whack of hammers as Gil and Oak covered over the broken window with an old piece of siding from the shed. They must have stayed in the parlour on watch because Elva lay awake all night and did not hear them come back up. Jane didn't sleep much either.

Amos had one of his attacks next morning. So violent in nature, Rilla drove into Demerett Bridge for the doctor.

It's a mystery to me, was all the field of medicine could offer. Amos would be bedridden for days.

Rilla, stuck with yet another bill, did the unthinkable.

"There's a room over the shed that can be fitted up nicely," she said to Gil and Oak. "No need for him to know."

THANKS TO LONGER DAYS, next evening found Elva behind the shed with Rilla, weeding the square patch of vegetables. She hated crawling and picking and swatting at blackflies, listening to Rilla say, Stop fussing, girl, you'll be thankful for potatoes come the fall. If they made it, thought Elva. What produce the squirrels and rabbits didn't scamper off with barely amounted to anything in soil that reeked of turpentine, of all things.

The worst about that damned chore for Elva was the black fingernails and why couldn't she at least wear gloves? She had a hell of a time getting that tarry soil out and Amos didn't want to see dirty hands at his table, but Rilla thought Elva was just being vain.

"Be sure to take that brush to you," Rilla said on the way into the summer kitchen.

She and Elva found Jane, Oak and the brothers Barthélemy standing awkwardly in the hallway by the front door. This is funny, thought Elva, nobody knowing that everyone knows. Rilla said they looked as if they been caught with their hands in the cookie jar and at least go out on the porch so Amos don't hear.

"Dom's brought news from town," said Jane.

Oak dragged maple porch chairs around for everyone. There weren't enough so he sat on the railing by Gil. Gil, quite innocently, moved beside Jane, Major dutifully following, Dom on the other side. Elva mentally weaved a daisy chain of who here feels what about whom, unable to keep track of everyone's secrets.

"Jane, cut up some of that leftover Simple Simon cake you made for the boys," said Rilla.

Jane wasn't much of a cook but her white sponge cake with brown sugar and butter icing was somewhat of a treat and Amos liked it to finish off a Sunday dinner because it was cheap to make. Rilla was allowing herself some good manners in the offer, since Amos passed out sick upstairs would be none the wiser. Jane just looked glad to be doing something.

That's not like her, thought Elva.

"Came from the church," Dom said. "Father Cértain wanted help boarding up the windows. He's worried about the stained glass."

"Are things that bad?"

"Oh yes, ma'am."

Dom stood and pulled the front page of the Halifax *Evening Mail* from his back pocket. It was a few days old, but the large photograph captured a man and woman being beaten with sticks. Knowing that Elva couldn't read, Rilla and Jane just barely, Dom delicately explained that rioters had dragged King Duplak and his wife into the street, kicked the shit out of him, roughed her up some, looted his emporium to emptiness, and kissed the storefront plate window with a great big rod of iron.

"Don't look like Mr. Duplak," Rilla said.

"Looks like it's a composograph," said Oak.

"A what?"

Jane returned with a plate of cake slices, the screen door banging after her.

"It's made up. Papers in the city do it all the time when they don't have a real picture. They take other pictures, cut pieces of them together and make one that fits the story."

"Doesn't seem like that's right."

Oak shrugged.

"Well, was he hurt?"

Dom couldn't say for sure, but the newspaper said the shopkeep had to be taken to a hospital in the city.

While Rilla wasn't particularly sorry about that, neither did she have a wish for any harm to come to King Duplak and couldn't understand why this had happened.

"It's the strikers, ma'am. Folks have been saying for years that Mr. Duplak sets his prices by what the Corporation tells him, and now with people having a hard time making ends meet, it was bound to happen. Especially now. Rumour is, they're going to truck in even more scabs and get the foundry up to full production."

No one was eating Jane's cake.

"What? What's wrong?" asked Dom.

"Gil's—"

"Shut up!" said Jane and she slapped Elva on the wrist.

"Well?"

Big long pause.

"I'm working at the foundry, Dom," Gil said.

"Jesus Christ! Are you nuts?"

While everyone else thought so, no one said.

"But why?"

"Money, what else?"

"Gil, they're going after anyone they even think is doing it. I came here to tell you to stay away from town, don't even go past the ponds. It's not safe."

Elva figured this visit was really for Dom to tell Jane, No more trips to the Abbey.

"Promise me you won't do it again. It's too dangerous. If they find you out, they'll come here."

"I'm afraid it's too late for that," Rilla said. She explained about the rock.

"Oh, Gil!"

Elva knew Dom was angry because Gil's actions jeopardized Jane, but Dom couldn't raise too much of a stink, could he?

"You have to stop," Dom said. "Please, Gil."

He excused himself by saying he had to get home, didn't like to leave his mother alone with so much unrest about. No chance for a private word with Jane. Amos was awake upstairs and shouting, Rilla!

"Warm me up some milk," she said to Jane, going inside. "Bring it up when it's ready."

There were flies now, on the untouched cake slices.

After Rilla made Gil explain to her the precautions being taken to keep scabs' identities secret—decoy buses, alternating which factory entrances they used, even paying off strikers to keep their mouths shut—she agreed to turn a blind eye. What choice did she have with Amos upstairs puking his guts out and shitting red? They'd just all have to continue to tread lightly and make sure the sick man didn't find out. But Jane and Elva were forbidden to leave Kirchoffer Place.

Like that was going to do any good. It's not fair, Jane chafed under house arrest, but exactly not fair to whom Elva didn't know. She knew that Rilla's admonishment to avoid town was losing potency with each day. Jane missed Dom, wanted him, and while his very reflection dogged her step in the house, it brought no solace. Just the opposite. She took out her frustration on Elva, flushing her out of her sight with tear-wringing pinches.

Elva wasn't the only one to suffer. Rilla, ever mindful of keeping food on the table and Amos alive—and consequently, the roof over head—barely noticed anything amiss in her daughter's behaviour. Wasn't that just Jane? Oak was different. He once had the misfortune to be holding a fresh cup of tea during one of her moody passes through the hall. Pardon, he begged, the tea splashing down onto his leg. Not a boo of complaint from Oak, although Elva later found him slathering a butter poultice on a large raised blister. He smiled gently, said that Jane scared the hell out of him and he missed having that tea.

If Elva and Oak got in Jane's way, Gil was getting at her heart. Of course Gil had to know that she was frustrated being apart from Dom, but rather than stay away from her, Gil seemingly taunted her. Hello, Jane, how'd you sleep? Can I get something for you, Jane? Shall I read to you, Jane? What would you like to listen to on the radio, Jane?

Don't I look like my brother, Jane!

To Elva, Jane should have been revelling in two brothers adoring her. And if she didn't care a fig for Gil, why not enjoy being his harmless fantasy? It's not like she was asking for his attention. Yet Gil's flattery enraged her. Elva couldn't figure it out. Nor could she understand why Jane did everything she could to stay in Gil's sights.

Nope. It just didn't make sense to Elva at all.

Rilla was desperate to get the man some relief and thought berries might settle Amos's stomach. She and Elva were out back.

"Gruson's Field. They ripen there first."

A hearty ocean wind blew the tall grass flat and gave the few scrappy alders in the yard a workout.

"They won't be ready," said Elva.

"Look for the higher plants. They get more sun."

"They'll be too small."

"They're the tasty ones."

Elva, not much help with heavier housework, had been delegated to pick strawberries. Amos liked them with his breakfast, said it helped to keep his food down. Although the afternoon was perfect for such a chore, the field was several miles away and no way was Elva going out there on her own.

"Gruson's Field is nowhere near town."

But what if, what if, what if . . .

"We'll just ask the berries to hold off ripening till the strike's over" pretty much summed up Rilla's thoughts on that. "Fine, then. The boys'll be home soon. Ask one of them to go with you."

Elva got her wooden basket and plunked herself down on the back stoop. Gil and Oak, their hours at the foundry irregular, soon came up the lane. They'd found it easier and safer to slip through a hole in the foundry fence and make their own way home rather than take the bus. Those strikers out for scabs by the gates wouldn't spare time for a couple of stragglers.

"Hey, Elva, what's up?"

"Gotta pick strawberries for him upstairs and I'm afraid to go by myself."

"We'll go with you," said Oak and he grabbed an empty Mason jar off the window sill.

Gil looked to the door. "Yeah, why not, eh?"

Oak, it turned out, was a consummate berry picker. Fast, delicate, stopping only now and then to stretch and gaze out over the low rolling meadow overlooking Cape Jeddore Head.

Gil would have none of that. He stripped off his sweat-stained coveralls and singing loudly about a waltzing Australian Matilda, he washed himself clean in a pool of rainwater collected in a mossy basin of bedrock. It was ice cold and made him scream, Aye

Nellie! Then he lazily spread himself on a carpet of lichen, his head resting on his hands. Overhead, white outraged faces were being pushed unceremoniously across the heavens while the Major tore after dragonflies.

"What? You've seen me naked before."

That was as a boy when they swam at the beach. He didn't know about the crack in the bedroom closet thing. This was different. Gil didn't care. Or he didn't care that it was Elva who saw. She thought Gil was looking mighty pleased with himself one minute, perplexed by a riddle the next.

"If you could have one wish, Elva, what would it be?" he said dreamily, Oak too far away to hear.

"To be Jane," she replied without thinking.

Gil sat up. Elva looked away from Gil quickly and went back to picking.

"Yeah? You know, I pretended to be my brother. Years ago. We only tried it the once. Dom got caught nippin' into the wine at church when he was an altar boy." From the look that got from Elva, Gil added quickly, "Now don't you ever let this out, you, or Dom'll skin me alive! It's our secret, okay?"

"What happened?"

"He got pissed is what happened. That crazy old Father Bourque marched him all the way home, goin' on about hell and sin and if you kiss a girl and something starts to stiffen, you're in mortal sin. Thought Maman was going to have a fit. Said when my father got home, Dom was going to get it. Belt, get it. Dom was throwing up all over the place saying, I'm sorry I'm sorry I'm sorry. Fun-ny!"

"Did he get it?"

"Naw, I took his place when my pappa got home."

"How come?"

"We both knew my old man would whip Dom some good with that belt of his. I wasn't going to let everyone in town see my brother looking beat up the next time he was serving Mass."

"Did they find out?"

"Sure, but by then, they'd calmed down some. Dom was okay." Then: "Why you, Elva? Why do you want to be Jane?"

She bent her face away, regretting she'd said anything.

"Elva, everyone's, well . . . crippled in some way, even Jane."

She wondered what he saw about Jane that was deformed. Even so. *Folks don't mind cripples if they're like Jane—or you—and you'll prefer anything over me, and always will. I know that, don't I, Gil?*

"Now me, I'd be one of those clouds. Not a thought in my head. Spending all day drifting about looking down on you lugs. I'd be in Barbados by dinner, Brazil by supper."

Oak, his jar filled, joined them.

"Ask him," said Elva.

"Ask me what?"

But Gil did not, deciding that no one, at least not Elva, needed to hear what Oak's wish would be.

Major began to bark.

"Someone's coming."

Gil stood up. "It's Dom. Where's he going?" He jumped into his clothes and ran into the field after him, Major barking wildly in pursuit. "I'll see you back at the house!"

"Anything to get out of picking berries, huh?" Oak said to Elva.

It was getting late. Oak bent out the kinks from being hunched over. The mosquitoes were starting to bite. They were partial to the young man, even more than Elva. She thought it was because he was tall and they'd get him first.

They said practically nothing as they walked home. Elva didn't mind. His silences weren't unnerving like Gil's or Jane's. When those two weren't talking, it was like something ready to erupt. Oak was just, simply, a quiet fellow. Comfortable. Like Major when he was curled up at his master's feet. That's why the blast startled them.

A short snap from the northeast, followed by a hollow roar and the resounding collapse of timbers. The sound travelled far and easily over the lake waters and the tar ponds and in the evening air. Elva knew the explosion was from a good distance and only when she saw the

smoke by the shores of Ostrea Lake did she know it had
come from Demerett Bridge.

When she turned to ask Oak what he thought it
was, she found him on his knees, trembling so hard that
his face glistened with tears that came from the sides of
his mouth. Two bright red patches appeared under his
eyes, and when he seized her hands, his were like ice.

"Would you get me back?" he managed, adding that
he'd be obliged if she didn't say anything about this to
anyone, especially to Gil.

As Elva helped Oak to his feet, she saw that he'd
wet himself.

RILLA SAID THE NOISE reminded her of the *White Bear* when the steamer gutted herself up the coast. She'd been a child when it happened, seventy-three passengers and crew spilling out like toy soldiers on the shoals at Chance Cove. She remembered driving out in the back of a horse-pulled wagon to see the wreck and someone, she wasn't sure who, giving her warm root beer. There were so many sightseers, it was like a Sunday picnic.

The explosion in Demerett Bridge was not as memorable as *White Bear*'s boilers shooting out hissing coal like Catherine wheels, but it destroyed the union headquarters on Pleasant Point Road, killing one man. With local resources already stretched by the strike, Halifax sent additional police to aid in the investigation. The conclusion: an incendiary device planted by someone well acquainted with the office layout. The official report pinned all blame on the victim, a union steward, claiming he set the bomb to win back waning public sympathy from a long and bitter strike, but something had gone wrong.

The union reacted swiftly, whipping up its membership by protesting that the police were nothing more than pawns of the Maritime Foundry Corporation. More capitalist corruption! Red flags began to flutter from rooflines and appear in arm bands. Just the spectre of Communist involvement in the dispute was enough for Province House in Halifax to send in more police. Lines of angry men faced off against uniforms on horseback. Those folks in Demerett Bridge not battling in the street stayed home, drew their blinds and wished it all away.

"How sweet." Amos laughed. "Serves that bloody Jew right." Yet again on the mend, he'd been catching up on the doings in town. He was most delighted to hear King

Duplak had been ruined, his windows, once the envy of the town, shattered by a mob, littering the street like crystal. "Only good thing to come out of this!"

Rilla said she saw Mr. Duplak and his wife at church and said she didn't think they were Jewish, but Shut up, woman, was all she got for that.

The early start to summer had brought unusually hot winds laced with fine caustic beach powder—gritty, gnawing, rubbing everyone's nerves raw like sandpaper. The troubles in town had not yet spilled over to the other side of the tar ponds only because there wasn't anything of value for either side in the dispute to burn or tear down.

Gil and Oak still poured iron, getting in and out of the factory by a meandering path through the tar ponds, always coming home with news of the day. Amos was pretty much in the dark about his boarders, and Elva wondered how long her mother, how long they all, could sustain the ruse. As long as he's sick in bed, Rilla would reply.

In the evenings after supper, Oak would spread his delicate precision tools on the kitchen table and quietly dissect a pocket watch. Not much of a talker, Elva thought he just wanted to avoid attention.

"Well, if you ask me, he's a duke or something. On the lam from, I dunno, whatever dukes do. A royal right here in our shitty little town. Maybe we should paint the outhouse."

Elva said she didn't ask, and that Jane was making fun of her, which she was. Rilla reminded Jane about the use of *shitty* and to stop talking like a gangster.

Conversely, Oak could be a murderer hiding out from the Mounties because he offed his ol' lady for her money.

Rilla had enough of Jane's speculation, thank you very much, and she was sure Oak didn't sit around trying to figure out who they were.

The situation was sort of like Oak himself, wanting to know what made those watches of his tick. He was able to see the gears and windup whatsits, but as to what made them go, well, that took some tinkering.

I think he just wants to be with Gil. Of course Elva didn't say that.

Equally hard to know if Gil wanted to be with Oak. Sometimes Gil would make a visit home, so he said. Rilla thought it right nice that he was trying to mend fences back there, but his friend left behind didn't seem too happy about it. Other times, Gil'd stretch out on the pile of firewood across from the summer kitchen, watching Oak at the table inside. Sometimes, of an evening, he'd stay there until Major curled up and all that remained of Gil was the red tip of his cigarette — thinking what? — while a few miles up the road, folks were killing each other over a few cents more in wages.

After the dishes were done, Elva and Jane helped Rilla with the washing. It's such a sight, Rilla might say, staring out the back door, thinking. The garden, such as it was, was overgrown. Sheds needed sorting. Siding was cracked and dry-rotting. Amos upstairs in bed. How were they going to make it?

Jane was thinking too and Elva knew what about. Why hadn't Dom come to visit? Why no word at all? Was he safe? Where was he?

There! Right there, through the screen door, only it wasn't Dom, was it? Just Gil, shirtless against the hot night wind. Sometimes he'd catch Jane watching him. He'd smile. Missing nothing. Then he'd see Elva.

Miss Nothing.

Elva! Oak was pulling her off the bed.

What's the matter? she asked, so sleepy. Where's my robe?

No time for that, c'mon, Elva!

What about Jane? She couldn't leave Jane.

There was smoke and Major was barking.

Jane's on the landing, hurry!

Thank God! Jane covered Elva with a blanket.

You can't leave him, Rilla was saying. Amos couldn't make the stairs.

Go! Gil shouted from below.

Oak set Elva down.

Cover your face! She and Jane went into the smoke.

Amos fell. Oak picked him up, too heavy! Rilla helped.

God almighty, where's the door!

They plunged into the blinding smoke, going down, following the sound of Gil's voice.

The boys got the fire out around dawn. As bad as it seemed, only Elva's favourite room was destroyed. The summer kitchen's roof had collapsed, taking with it the north wall siding. Ditto the pantry and laundry tubs. Weeks of airing, a couple of coats of paint, and the rest of the house would be back to normal.

Amos was lying on the front lawn, still coughing, going on about broken windows and how that Gil Barthélemy was a fucking scab, that this was his fault and how'd he fix Rilla for deceiving him. By Christ, he'd show her!

"Things don't look good, boys," Rilla said to Gil and Oak.

"Damn sorry about this. We're done with the foundry," Gil said.

Rilla agreed that it was probably best.

Oak was kicking into a pile in the driveway the last few smouldering timbers. The deep blue of early dawn was quickly yielding. Jane, quietly, wanted to know what they were going to do.

"Can't stay. Not now."

Even after what had just happened, Rilla was reluctant to agree. Her man lying in the front yard and she wouldn't even be able to get him back inside, let alone up the stairs.

"If they're not working any more, no one'll bother us," said Elva.

Rilla looked hopeful. The money be damned, she needed help, and even after this incident, she still felt safer with the boys around.

Gil shook his head. "Too risky. I'll go back to my mother's place."

Jane said, Good idea, but they all knew what kind of reception he could expect from Jeanine.

"But Oak can stay, can't he?" said Elva.

No point in both Gil and his friend suffering the wrath of Jeanine Barthélemy, so, Yeah, why not? That would be just fine, said Rilla. Jane didn't care. Sure Oak was odd, all loosey-goosey over a loud noise one day, saving them from fire the next, but Elva'd miss him, like a roof beam holding up something, even if he didn't say much and Oak right now looked as if Elva had just cut off his right arm. But it was settled. Even weak-as-a-kitten Amos had to agree it was for the best.

ELVA WAS IN THE PROPER KITCHEN cleaning a
bowl of anaemic radishes she'd spent all afternoon
gleaning from the mucky garden. Jane took over the
other end of the table with a writing tablet and pencil.

"Go on, get out," she said.

In this state, it was always best to ignore Jane.

"You deaf now as well as ugly?"

Elva pulled a face.

Jane had precious little schooling, which was considerably more than Elva. That was Amos's doing. C'mon now, he told Rilla. She couldn't expect the kids in that church school that taught the half-breeds like Jane to look at Elva, on account of her being deformed and all. Put them right off their learnin'. Have some sense, woman! If nothing else, Amos was pragmatic.

Elva kept her eyes on the radishes. Jane's writing was laborious, her letters uneven and childlike. Repeated attempts were accompanied by tearing of paper, frantic erasures, snorts and Jesus Christs! Just what the hell was she up to? Of course Elva was dying to know, but furtive glances would have to do. She knew better than to ask. Or even look like she was interested. Then after a long silence Elva sensed she was being watched.

"You need some fresh air."

"You know what Rilla said."

"Arsehole! Who'd hurt you?"

"I'm afraid."

"You're a fraidy-ass, then."

"Am not."

"Prove it. Take this to Dom."

"No!"

Jane grabbed her arm and pinched it until Elva cried out, "You're hurting me!"

"Do it."

"Why don't you?"

"'Cause of that mother of his. Puts me right off. Might whomp her one of these days."

"What do you want to tell Dom?" Elva wanted to add, More lovey-dovey stuff? But she figured Jane would skin her alive if she told.

"None of your fucking business. And if you tell anyone about this I'll drop an earwig into your tea and make you drink it. Then you'll have earwig babies."

Elva doubted the earwig baby thing, but she knew her life would be a living hell until she did her sister's bidding. "And don't get it creased, hold it proper now," followed Elva out the door.

What Elva didn't count on was the effect the pile of charred wood in the driveway had on her—images of hordes of rioters, bearing torches, tying her to a stake, lighting matches between her toes like Joan of Arc—

"Go!" shouted Jane from the window.

When Elva was far enough out of her sister's sight, she plunked herself down in the grass, what if-ing until she had to blink back the tears. Maybe she could just throw the damn piece of paper away and say she'd given it to Dom? Or say some bird ate it. Who'd know? Then—

Rustling, something darting, panting, towards her. Major jumped into her arms, licked her startled face.

"Hey, Elva. What are you doing in the grass? Looks like you've seen a ghost. Oak around?"

"You . . . scared . . . me. He's . . . working . . . in the shed."

"What's wrong?"

All she could do was wave the note.

"Jane wants me to take this . . . to Dom. But I'm afraid to go to your place by myself. What if someone catches me? And your mother? I know she doesn't like me. What if she sees me talking to Dom?"

"Her, I wouldn't worry about. She's too hoppin' mad having me around, and that's only 'cause Dom said I had to come home or he'd talk to the priest about her turning away her own son. Hell, these days, Maman wouldn't even notice you."

She giggled at the notion of Jeanine Barthélemy hopping. Gil sure had picked up some odd turns of phrase in Halifax.

"What's it say?"

Elva shrugged.

"I'll take it, then."

"Oh no!" Elva slipped the note into the pocket of her apron.

"Jane won't know," Gil said, his hand wiping the tears from her face and sweeping down under her chin. "C'mon."

But that just wouldn't be right.

"Which pocket is it in, Elva?" Gil grabbed for her, tickling her, rolling her over, tickling her some more. "Give it up, where is it?"

"No!" she giggled in delight, that spilling desperate-to-get-out hiccuping exuberance. "Gil!"

He had her pinned. So close, she inhaled the cedar fishing shed near his home and its oakum and his sweat. Elva allowed herself to remember: just like Dom and Jane.

Gil held up the note.

"Aha! The lady gives up her treasure! But don't worry, Elva. I'll say you fought me to the bitter end."

"Give it back! Jane won't like it."

"Don't tell her, stupid, and she won't ever find out."

"Please, Gil!"

But Gil had whistled for Major and was striding back to his place. "No need to thank me! I'll be sure Dom gets it! And Elva, you should laugh more often."

Jane was waiting in their room. *Snap ∫nap ∫nap* went the pages of Elva's colouring book. She wasn't even looking at the pictures as she leafed through it. Elva peered around the door. She'd stayed outside long enough to make Jane think she had walked to Dom's and back.

"Hey! That's mine."

"Here, then. What do I care about your stupid bird pictures. Did he get it?"

Elva nodded.

"Well? Got one for me?"

Elva shook her head.

Amos passed in the hall clutching a white enamelled bowl, heading back to the shitter.

THAT STRANGE WEATHER BEGAN on a June day, bright, blustery, with thick bands of purple streaming across the horizon. Then the wind shifted from the north, bringing with it a dull silvery hue. And cold. A hanging-like-balls-of-fog-in-front-of-your-mouth kind of cold. Even Rilla had to stop in the middle of pinning laundry in the backyard. She had never seen or felt the like before and said so, in her native tongue, something she rarely did since the devout Sisters of Infinite Charity tried to beat the Indian out of her with rulers across the knuckles. By twilight, purple skies had inked out the stars and given way to low racing clouds. Prelude to a gale.

Rilla had the holy water out, reserved for thunderstorms and hurricanes. Whatever was coming warranted a little God-protecting dab on the forehead. Elva did so reverently. Oak politely declined the offer to cross himself with water, blessed or otherwise, and Elva realized she had no idea what god, if any, he prayed to. Jane rolled her eyes and Rilla said, fine then and if the house blows down she'll be the only one killed and did she want that? From the way she'd been acting of late, Jane probably didn't care.

When no reply came to her letter, Jane's routine became a languid and listless march from the parlour radio, where she'd listen for a few hours — Amos too ill to drag himself out of bed — to a mopey survey of a world made up of tar ponds from her bedroom window. Rilla, too busy to notice anything, kept saying Jane was just a lazy arse spoiled thing.

Elva knew that was only partly it. Unforgivably, Dom was ignoring Jane. No one knew better than Elva how that treatment would fester. At least she thought she did. But there were no fireworks and rants and fits on a grand scale. Just Jane braiding long grass as she wandered up behind the house, like she was waiting for someone. Elva'd wrap her arms about her knees and watch from the porch, wondering if she should tell their mother, Jane's perishing from a broken heart! Hunger would drive Elva to tea and toast long before the perishing bit got too far.

Oak had been occupying his days either with tearing away the remains of the summer kitchen, piling the debris neatly in the back of the garden, or cleaning out the shed.

"That's a fine idea," Rilla said. "If I can park the truck inside, I can load the washing at night and get me a few more minutes in the morning."

Then every evening after the dishes had been cleared, he'd sit at the round table with the light bright overhead and watch his watches. If he'd been studying for a test, Elva was sure he'd pass it hands down.

Rilla and her girls had been in the parlour listening to a Halifax fiddling contest from the Lord Nelson Hotel, Elva wrapped in a quilt against the unseasonable cold. Amos had taken another turn. White enamelled pail in tow, he'd limped up to bed early. The wind had been rattling the windows all evening and the electric lights flickered out. That's that, said Rilla, and Jane followed her up to bed. Elva decided to wait until moody Jane was asleep before crawling in next to her and went to see what Oak was up to in the kitchen.

He'd just lit the oil globe hanging over the table and

the room was bathed in humming amber warmth.
Summer moths, not knowing what in tarnation was
going on with this kind of weather, flew too close to
the hot lamp, then flopped groggily around the sugar
bowl. Oak didn't seem to notice Elva slipping into
the chair beside him. A bee was crawling across the
oilcloth, too cold to fly. Elva flicked at it with her
forefinger just as the dainty screw in Oak's hand
slipped its mark.

"Oh, for the love of Christ!"

Oak threw it. The pocket watch bounced off the
table, shattered, a fragment hitting Elva over the eye.
He groaned and went outside.

"Can't be fixed," he said.

He wasn't really talking to her but searching the
night-darkened surf restless and angry somewhere
nearby. Elva covered in her patchwork quilt had joined
him by the pile of charred wood.

"You've fixed all kinds of things."

"I went to see Gil this afternoon. He told me not to
come by any more."

Oak absentmindedly started on the path towards
the Barthélemy farm.

"Why?"

"We fought. About her."

"Jane?"

"Dom took a job on a fishing boat, out of
Musquodoboit Harbour. Gone for three months, maybe

longer. Says he needed the money to marry Jane, take her away from here."

Oh!

"It was kinda last minute and Dom didn't have a chance to see Jane and tell her. He asked Gil to."

"How come Jane doesn't know?"

"Because Gil won't tell her!"

"Why not?"

He touched her forehead. "You're bleeding. I'm sorry, Elva. I shouldn't have said anything. I don't know what's the matter with me."

She'd stolen all his secrets, and forgot that she shouldn't know. "You love him."

Elva could only imagine the terror on a face by night she could not see. Oak looked around, cleared his throat.

"I can't."

"But you do," she persisted.

"What I do is hurt!" He groaned again, holding his stomach. "Just hurt. All the time. Hurt! Does that . . . disgust you?"

She shook her head.

He studied her. "Why not?"

Elva couldn't say. Like it was natural in her, knowing that for some, it was the way of things.

"And you think Gil loves Jane and not you."

"What?" he asked, unsure if there wasn't a hundred years of wisdom hiding in that little deformed body.

"He *thinks* he loves her. It's not that he doesn't care for me, he doesn't want to care. He fights caring. I know he's out there right now, just as I'm here with you, fighting against it . . . fighting against me. Love Jane? Not a chance! Jane's what's expected. Jane is easier. Gil wants escape, to be Dom and have everything that belongs to Dom. Being Dom means not being Gil, undoing things, not being . . ."

Gil was thirteen when Oak met him; the *Meghan Rose* had sunk a few months before. Filthy, hungry, he was still the most beautiful boy Oak'd ever seen on the streets of Halifax. He knew nothing about big-city ways, been begging around the waterfront for work and had been eating out of the garbage bins behind a diner. At night, he slept under the table-like tombstones in St. Paul's Cemetery across from the lieutenant governor's mansion, but with fall coming and the stevedores saying early ice meant a hard winter, Gil was worried about what to do.

Oak kept an eye out for boys like him, cajoled them with offers of a warm place to stay, something to eat, befriended them; he did those things for a man named Bryant Slaunwhite. Oak himself had been recruited, at an even younger age than Gil. All you have to do is close doors in your head to places you don't want to go, he'd tell Gil later, advice Gil could never follow. Oak had been one of Bryant's best boys, but the man's customers were a hard-drinking, hard-wearing lot and there was always a demand for younger, fresh talent.

Oak took Gil to Bryant's place, the Seadog Tavern on Barrington Street, down towards the docks. Very popular with the navy lads. You won't mind it one bit, he said. At least it's warm and there's a square meal in it for you. For all the advance billing Oak gave it, the Seadog Tavern was a cellar where high tide often left two inches of fish-reeking water on the floor.

As Oak knew he would be, Bryant was taken with the good-looking country boy, fixed him up with a job flogging gin because he figured he'd hold his own. But Gil didn't take to it, told Oak that the Seadog Tavern wasn't regular, all those innuendoes and leering glances from men — it wasn't right.

Gil bolted the first time the place got raided. Oak knew where to find him, it not being hard as Gil had nowhere to go. Raids like that happen all the time, Oak said. Nothing to worry about. Bryant pays the cops to leave him be. It was just the way men like Bryant had to do business down in the docks. And pay no mind to what the regulars say. They're just in their cups funnin' ya when they talk about wantin' to suck your dick. C'mon. Come back.

And for once, Oak wasn't pretending to be a friend to the new kid around. He liked Gil, and their friendship from the get-go was genuine.

"Hey, thanks," Gil said when Oak gave him the watch.

Oak had found the broken timepiece in the bar. Said he had a knack for fixing them.

"My father had one like this. Like his dad's. But he lost it when . . ."

Oak said he should get over the sinking.

"How can I? It was up to me to be watching the weather. Not drinking coffee and sleeping."

Oak said that coffee kept him awake.

"It's my fault, Oak! After that mast went down, they had to cut my old man's legs off when they took him off the wreck. You don't know what that was like for him."

"I've seen worse." But Oak didn't say how.

"Don't think poorly of me for it, do you?"

"No."

"Guess I'm lucky. And thankful for what Mr. Slaunwhite's done for me. I'll make a few bucks and then I'm out of here."

"Gil, be careful."

"Of what?"

"Bryant. He's, well, he's into a lot of things. He's not the sort of man you want to cross."

"If you mean he's a bootlegger, I figured that out."

"Then you'll understand he never takes no for an answer."

Bryant had been very persuasive in making sure Oak understood that Gil owed, and was owned by, Bryant.

"There's money in it, Gil. Lots of money," Oak said. "More than you've ever had. Just one or two blokes a night. Set yourself up in no time, then get away from here and no one ever knows."

"You're fucking crazy!"

"Just close your eyes and don't think about it. It's over before you know it. A few months' work and you can do whatever you want."

But truth was, Bryant would never let Gil go, and Oak knew that.

Gil knew all about pork-bellied shopkeepers slobbering into their brew before slobbering over you. They had it in Demerett Bridge, but it was the lot of women, and women thought most unkindly of. Women like Elva's mother. Stained women. Once they were stained, there was no going back, never getting it out. And a man to act that way? Just what would that make him? No way! No how.

Away from the regular clientele, in a small brick-lined room upstairs, Bryant and a couple of his best boys pushed Gil up against the wall and Bryant raped him. He called it a love tap, saying there'd be a lot more after him, but he'd make sure Gil remembered his first. And this: for each time he said no to Bryant, he'd lose a finger. After that, Gil could pick which body part came off next.

The only thing Gil ever said to Oak about it was that while Bryant did him, he watched a roach hiding in the mortar between the bricks, twitching its antennae, staring up at him as if to say, And you think I'm nothing. For a long time after that, Gil hated Oak for drawing him into this world.

Gil stopped talking about running. There'd been boys who'd run before. They'd find parts of them in the harbour. Bryant had no choice about that. His rent boys knew too much about smuggling gin and cocaine and which customs officials were getting the payoff. And of course there were the customers, who'd just as easily have sliced the giblets out of Bryant as his boys to keep the white marble stoops of their domestic reputations unsullied. So who cared a goddamned about dead nancies who let their arses out by the quarter hour? Didn't even make the papers unless some politico was making hay by cleaning up street vermin.

But Oak knew that Gil was thinking about it just the same. In fact, there was precious little Gil said even though he and Oak were locked up together after each night for the next five years. The hatred eventually gave way, eroded mostly by Oak's feelings for Gil. Oak was never fooled as to how Gil came around. Close quarters, shared sympathies after a licking from Bryant, reading together on cold winter nights. Take your pick. But not love. Not at first. More like a yielding that meant more to one, nothing to the other. Oak wondered how men could come round night after night and find pleasure in an act when one of the players was absent in every way that mattered. And he wished Gil would come back. They shared a bed but it was like Gil was not even there. Instead, there was a face creased with self-loathing and contempt, a mind feverishly planning, always waiting for an opportunity.

It came during the distraction of loading a schooner. It was to be the largest cargo of spirits Bryant had ever planned to run past the customs blockade outside Boston. He had the bottles of gin and rum packed in crates marked as Bibles.

Oak was with the first crew back from loading the ship. One of Bryant's boys was sitting on the tavern steps. Sniffling, he pointed inside to where Bryant was, face down behind the bar. A rowing oar mounted for decoration behind the gin bottles had been taken to his face, scattering his teeth about like stars. No need to wonder who'd done it. Gil was gone. Last thing Oak heard before he went AWOL too was that Bryant, who had friends in the Halifax police, had sworn a warrant against Gil.

They stood before the blackness of night, breathing in harmony, shivering. Elva was feeling very grownup.

"Hear that?" Oak said. "It's gotten real quiet."

"What about that fella, he okay?"

"Bryant? He's alive. Probably wished he wasn't. Bryant was right big on his looks."

They were standing by the shore at the end of the slate road by Kirchoffer Place. The wind had ceased.

Oak swiped a handful of pebbles and cast them one by one into the placid water. Then they were silent for a long while.

"I . . . I never thanked you. For not saying anything . . . you know."

Elva guessed Oak meant about Gruson's Field.

"My folks were killed in the Halifax explosion. Baby sister too. I was delivering newspapers. Came to under a bathtub. It saved me. I have trouble with loud noises now. I'm okay if I know they're coming. It's when I don't, well . . . Son of a bitch!"

It was snowing.

AN EERIE SILVER IRIDESCENCE bathed the room as Elva lurched sleepily towards the window, then flinched from the glare. From down the hall, Amos was yelling, What in Christ is going on with the weather? Brilliant white snow covered the black top of the tar ponds, crushed the fields of seagrass, weighed down the pink blossoms on the primrose bushes and clung tenaciously to the drooping green-leaved tree branches. Only something this magical would cause Elva to forget what she had to tell Jane about Dom.

At breakfast, which Jane barely touched and over which Rilla hovered, there was no chance to say, Hey, Jane, Dom wants to marry you and he's working on a fishing boat to save money and won't his ma be pissed off with the both of you when she finds out? With that snow out there, who cared if Oak didn't show for breakfast and Rilla said if you go out, take Elva, it's safer and don't go near town.

The morning sun was already working on dispelling whatever cosmic oops had conspired to turn the sixth month into December. Seven village children waving driftwood festooned with frozen kelp whirled in unison on the distant breakwater. Others were singing "Jingle Bells" all the way into making snow angels by the beach. With so many folks about making light of ankle-deep snow while being dressed for summer, Rilla's concern seemed overdone.

"We're not supposed to go near town," Elva said when she realized where Jane was heading.

"I'm not."

"Why so fast?"

"You're slow. That's not my fault."

A distant dog was barking the untie-me-please bark.

"You're going to the Abbey!"

Jane said she wasn't.

A lie, and Elva didn't have to wait until they got to the lake to know that. The ruins, usually with exploding colours and wrapped under the weighty boughs of emerald foliage, appeared to float disembodied through frothy clouds. The island was releasing itself from its earthly confines, slowly returning to heaven.

"Rilla said—"

"Shut it, Elva, will ya!"

She could have responded that she knew what was up with Jane. Something to do with that letter, Elva figured. Maybe Jane hoped to meet Dom again, but *he's not here.*

"Jane, I have to tell you—"

"Can't you shut up even for a minute? I'm going over there and you're staying here."

"Rilla said to stay together."

Jane only got angrier when Elva sulked; she hated to be reminded that Elva had feelings.

"Fine! What did you want to say?"

But Elva did have feelings and they'd been hurt. To hell with telling Jane about Dom, then. Easily enough remedied. Jane pushed her into the snow and slipped barefoot into the water.

Elva waited until her sister had disappeared into the trees on the other side, then she followed. The water was stinging, but Jane be damned, Elva wasn't going to miss seeing the Abbey like this and so what if she spied on Jane again. Serves that Jane right.

Ipswich Abbey was a remarkable place at any time of year, but ice-crystal-covered grottoes and cloisters, stone paths frozen into mirrors and icicles made Elva almost forget about Jane. As the June air melted the snow, Elva gathered frozen blossoms, made a snow angel that looked like a gnome and ate handfuls of snow until her head ached and she heard their voices.

"Every morning I've been here waiting, at the same hour," he said. "Since I got your note."

Elva had not realized she was so close to them, separated only by a clotted row of shrubs. She worked her way into the branches, having to dance out the snow that fell down the back of her dress, until she could see Jane smother his face with kisses.

"This was the first morning I could get away," Jane said. "My mother thinks there won't be much union trouble 'cause of the snow. She made me bring you-know-who, though. As if that thing would be any help if I got into trouble."

"Where is she?"

She wrapped her arms about his neck and laid her head against his chest.

"Don't you worry about Elva. Ditched her way back."

His large hand reached behind Jane's head and easily cradled it. He dropped his mouth to hers.

Jane pulled away.

"What?" He held her but she resisted.

"You can't fool me."

"Jane, don't."

"Gil, let me go!"

Jane clawed. A short scream fanned across the placid waters of the lake.

"Be quiet!" Gil slapped her, then dragged her down into the snow. "Oh Jesus, I didn't mean to—"

"Don't, please don't!"

He tossed off his shirt.

"Gil, why?"

"I have to . . . you know I do."

"Dom'll kill you for this!"

Gil pressed down on her, covering her, entangling himself in the idea of her to the tearing of fabric and rapid short breaths. Jane turned her face away from Gil's body and saw under the snow-covered green the brown-strapped shoes, the sagging socks, the twisted face watching her. Elva receded into the shrubs, confused by words that didn't match actions, the call for help that never came.

He was supposed to be mine, she thought. *Mine.*

She'd seen that look on Jane before, on someone else.

Jane lay motionless. Was she breathing? Her eyes were open and, thank god, she blinked. Gil wearily struggled into his clothes and stumbled into the trees, stopping once to glance back and throw up. Elva thought he was crying. Jane rolled on her side, clutching her dress, and saw Elva still squatting under the bushes.

Now she reached out a hand. "Get me home."

It took some doing, Elva being her crutch, stopping only when Jane faltered. They did not speak. It took them a very long time. When the reached the fields skirting the tar ponds, Jane collapsed.

"Say nothing. Ever. Swear!"

Elva couldn't speak. Why wasn't Jane angry? Across the road, Rilla got into the truck and pulled out of the laneway. Laundry run.

"Swear!"

Jane believed her sister was beyond jealousy, because Jane could not comprehend that crippled and ugly Elva was capable of feeling anything, least of all the sting of passion.

"Okay," said Elva.

The last few steps to the house were the hardest for Elva, fading fast under the weight of her sister's ordeal.

"Get me upstairs," Jane said on the porch, "and don't let Amos hear."

Melting snow was dripping from everything, everywhere. Their clothes were soaked, Jane's torn.

"Bury them in the garden," she said after Elva helped her into bed.

Elva did as she was instructed, then crawled in beside her sister to warm her. Then out it came, a torrent of I knew about Dom being away, Oak knew, and

I tried to tell you I really did but the snow and the letter to Gil, but he promised, he promised to give it to Dom and Dom on a fishing boat, hiccup, hiccup, and he wants to marry you.

"I'm sorry! It's my fault!" Elva was sobbing, hardly comprehending her own words.

Jane was not at all angry. Something else. Elva remembered where she'd seen that look on her sister's face before. Pleasure from pain. Gil and Oak.

Jane with Gil had been the same as Gil with Oak.

IN AUGUST OF 1927, the American owners of the Maritime Foundry Corporation issued its manager, Urban Dransfield, with this ultimatum: blacken the skies over Demerett Bridge with smelter smoke or sell the damned foundry. Dransfield's subsequent actions resulted in the second and unquestionably worse riot related to the strike.

The Corporation would later claim Dransfield acted on his own when he fired all the striking workers and then put out word that he was hiring—at half the former salary. There were enough destitute men out there, some from as far away as New Brunswick, that the employment call produced a line at the gate over a thousand men strong. Many of these men had been former employees unable to feed their families any longer on union platitudes, watching scabs take their jobs anyhow. But Dransfield's victory was short-lived.

The strikers' bitterness exploded in the Corporation's compound. Dransfield ordered buses, windows sealed over with plywood, to break up the riot by driving recklessly through the crowd. Dozens were maimed. Enraged strikers stormed and rocked the buses, overturning several. When Dransfield ordered his security guards to fire over the crowd, three men were accidentally shot. The gate and main offices were overrun. Dransfield was dragged into the compound and beaten and would later die from his injuries.

Demerett Bridge had had enough. The government agreed. Now it was a war, and troops, in the form of constabulary from all over the Maritimes, were sent in to restore order. All this, and in a few short years, no one would even remember why it began.

"I'm still head of this house," Amos said, leaning against the door jamb, looking shrunken and old.

They had become so accustomed to his absences that a place at supper was no longer set.

"What are you two crows staring at?" He sat across the table from Jane and Elva.

Rilla rose with an apology and fitted out a plate for him. Amos dumped it on the floor.

"Let that be a lesson to you, woman." He handed back the empty plate. "Fill it again."

She did, without protest, and set it in front of him.

"Now clean the floor."

Rilla moved.

"Not you. Her." Meaning Jane.

"I don't mind," said Rilla, but as she bent to clear away the food, Amos shoved her ass and she fell against the cupboards.

"Girl, clean the floor."

Rilla stood. "Amos, please."

"On your knees and wash that goddamn floor."

"No."

"Jane, please, like he says," Rilla said.

"No."

"Look at her," he said to Rilla. "Christ, but that little bitch hates me." Amos sat back and laughed. Watching Jane, he took a bite of his food, grimaced and spit.

"Christ, woman, you trying to kill me with that spicy shit and my punk gut?"

He spun the plate against the wall, bringing Oak, hammer in hand, from the summer kitchen.

"What the fuck do you want?"

"Nothing," Rilla said, anxiously looking for Oak to do just that.

Amos grumbled, same old song about it being that Barthélemy's goddamned fault the house got torched in the first place.

"It's all right," said Rilla, nodding her champion out of the room. Oak reluctantly went back to work.

"What's with that toady motherfucker anyway? Gives me a chill."

"You don't look right, Amos. Maybe you should be in bed."

"Oh, you'd like that, wouldn't you? Me outa your hair so you and this bunch can act like you own the place."

Rilla wiped her hands against her dress as she went about cleaning the mess. Damn! Gravy had seeped in between the floorboards. Now the ants would come.

"Do that later. Bring me something I can eat. And stop staring at me, you little bitch. You've been a moody puss for weeks. Yeah, I've seen you mooning about like a sick dog! Isn't it enough I'm off my food?"

Don't look, Elva told herself. Rilla put a fresh plate in front of Amos.

"He'd better be paying his board, Rilla."

The sound of hammering resumed. Amos pushed his food around with a fork. Jane looked as if she was trying to burn a hole through him with her eyes as Rilla filled a washbucket.

"What?"

"Nothing," Jane said.

"What's the matter with you?"

"Nothing."

What did you say? Nothing? What Gil did to you and you're supposed to marry Dom and Oak doesn't know what Gil did and I know he doesn't 'cause he's my friend now and he'd say for sure and you won't say what Gil did and make me swear not to tell . . . But Elva just took another mouthful of peas and no one noticed.

"Not eating? You were hungry enough when I took you in. You weren't so high and miss mighty then."

Rilla glanced up nervously. "Leave her, Amos, she's not well."

"What's wrong with her?"

His own bedridden decline made it easy for him to dismiss the inner torment, and sinking, of Jane. Her colour was waxy, her temperament listless. Bones had replaced shoulders and hips, and her once luxurious hair was falling out in handfuls.

"She's got the 'fluenza." Elva wanted to spare Jane any more scrutiny.

"My goddamn sorry arse she has. Eat, goddamn you!"

Jane said no, but the imploring gaze from Rilla down on the floor convinced her that it would be prudent for all if she at least tried. In went a spoonful of beans and peas, up it came, and out went Jane into the hall.

"The bitch did that on purpose," Amos said as Jane returned, somewhat unsteadily.

"No, she didn't," Elva said. "Jane's sick like that a lot."

"Shut it, Elva," said Jane.

Amos put his fork down. "I'll be some goddamned! That bitch whore's got herself knocked up."

And Elva knew it too.

Rilla pulled her hands out of the washbucket, slumped against the lower cupboard like her body had turned to water, Jane's silence confirming her worst fears. Oak hammered away obliviously outside.

"Fuck me blind," Amos cursed, slowly standing. "Whose is it?"

Jane stepped out of his way.

"No, Amos!" Rilla got a smack to the face with his elbow.

He lunged again.

"I should have beaten the fuckin' crap out of you a long time ago, you ungrateful slut! Make me a laughing-stock, will you? I'll throw your sorry arse back into the street where you belong. Christ, you goddamn Indians can't keep your legs crossed!"

Elva got shoved out of the way. Nothing more.

"Don't touch me!"

Amos overreached and fell, catching his side on the table edge. His face blanched with pain as he went down to hollering garbled fragments of sounds. The upset brought Oak back through the screen door.

Rilla was instantly by Amos's side, pulling her man's head into her lap, dabbing the spit from his chin with her apron. Elva had never seen convulsions before, trembling one moment, then like the man's arms and legs were being pulled out in opposite directions. He'd gone very pale, with little blue patches at the corners of his mouth, his eyes rolling back and forth into their pits.

Only Jane was calm, and she knelt, bending low to Amos's ear.

"Hurts, doesn't it?"

Something that might have been, Oh Christ, came out of the man.

"You can't imagine how you'll suffer, like we've all suffered for years. But don't worry. Your liver's turned to stone. Soon you'll be dead."

His eyes flared, but Amos had lost the ability to speak. Rilla had not. "Girl, what are you saying?"

"Rat poison in the milk."

"Sweet Holy Virgin, what have you done?"

"Stopped him from beating the shit out of you."

Now it looked as if Rilla would collapse.

"We'll have nothing . . . nothing," she said, more to herself. "You've ruined it! All this, everything I put up with, I did it for you."

"For me? I had to listen to him paw at you like some animal, night after night. For me? How long do you think it would be before he went from your bed to mine? Look, I'm younger, prettier. Then it would be for me, all right. Thank Jesus Elva's a cripple."

Tremors overtook Amos. He grabbed Jane and tried to pull himself up or her down.

"Let go of me." Jane stood defiantly against her mother.

Elva went to Oak's side.

"How long have you been doing this?" Rilla asked.

"Months."

"Will he recover?"

"He'd better not."

"Elva, go upstairs," said her mother.

Not a chance.

Oak asked if he should take the truck into town for a doctor.

"No," said Rilla. "No doctor."

"What are we going to do?" asked Jane.

"Shut it, girl!" Then Rilla gently laid Amos's head down and stood up. "I could use your help," she said to Oak.

He nodded without hesitation.

"Front room, his desk, there's paper. Get some to write with."

Oak ran to his errand and Rilla intercepted yet another convulsion.

"Amos, you're going to die," Rilla said with more firmness towards him than Elva or Jane had ever heard her use before. "Do you understand?"

She held him, rocked him, until his trembling passed, and then he nodded meekly.

"You got to make your life right before God. Nod if you understand."

Perhaps he thought he could buy himself hope, or more time, or even salvation by agreeing with her. He managed a weak sign.

Oak came back with paper and a pen.

"I want it legal and proper. Write that he leaves everything to me."

"Ma'am?"

"Do it!"

Amos groaned, his eyes wide. Oak pulled out a chair from the table, sat, and hastily scribed the will. When he was done, he read back to Rilla, I, Amos Stearns, being free to do so, leave everything to Rilla Twohig.

"How's that?"

Rilla nodded, then, "You owe me that, Amos."

Oak gave the paper to Rilla. Jane, sombre in triumph, was already looking down on the man as if he were in his grave.

"Is he really going to die?" asked Elva. No one answered. *But he's my father.*

Rilla put the pen into the man's hand and said, "Sign it." He could not. "Damn you, Amos, sign it." She took his hand and tried to help. "I can't do it."

"Give it to me," said Oak.

"No, it's not right."

"I know," he said. Oak took Amos's hand and the pen and signed the will. "If anyone asks, I witnessed his signature. It'll be better for you that way."

Rilla nodded.

Amos died there on the kitchen floor shortly after, his bowels eliminating in one last act of contempt.

ELVA SAW HIM coming up the driveway through snapping squares of white and white-long-past-white.

"What is it?" asked Rilla, expecting Elva to hand her another clothespin.

Oak saw him too. He was putting up the storm windows. Earliest they ever got up, said Rilla. She was some thankful Oak was still around to help out. September was blowing in cold, but dry.

"Hey," said Dom, dropping his duffel bag. His face was berry brown from the sun and wind. "Just got in."

Rilla resumed her pinning. "Expect your mother will be happy to see you."

Oak stood balanced on the ladder, holding a window, watching like he couldn't quite get his head around the twin thing. Feel one thing for one version, nothing for the other.

"I'm on my way. Thought I'd say hello first."

To Jane? We all know about it, Dom. But Elva kept that in her head.

"That's nice of you," said Rilla.

"Where's Gil?"

"Thought it best your mother wasn't alone out there these days."

"Heard things were bad. Still no settlement?"

Nobody bothered to answer.

Dom grinned. "That can't be going well. For Gil, I mean."

"Expect your mother's more worried about being alone than being with him." Elva always thought her mother had a hard look about her, but it was never harder than when she continued on doing something, like hanging wet socks, talking but not looking at you, like she did now with Dom. "And Jane's not here."

Elva thought even with the tan, Dom paled.

"She's helping out her aunt."

Help indeed. More like she'd been sent packing in the hopes that no-nonsense Auntie Blanche, even more no-nonsense than Rilla if you can believe that, might talk some sense into the girl. Not eating, not sleeping, walking around with Amos's white enamelled bowl, puking all the time; if anyone could put a stop to Jane tearing herself apart, it was Rilla's sister.

"When's she coming back?"

"Day or two."

"Then is Amos, I mean Mr. Stearns, here?" Dom had gotten right serious. "There's something I have to talk to him about."

Rilla stopped pinning. "He's dead."

"Jesus! I knew he'd been sick. When?"

"Couple of months back."

"Really sorry about that."

Rilla was pinning again. "What did you want with him?"

"Well, I, I'd hoped to talk to Jane first, but seeing as how things are." Dom looked awkwardly at the audience on the ladder and holding Rilla's clothespins. "I wanted to ask his, yours I guess, permission to marry Jane. I've made some money, not much but I've got a job lined up in Sydney and enough to get us there."

"That would be all right, Dom, considering how Jane's having your baby."

How'd she know? Elva wondered. Even after they'd buried Amos next to Dotsie, Jane refused to give up who the father was.

"That's that," said Rilla. "Didn't know for sure, Jane not saying, but from the look on ya, you figure it's yours too."

"Does . . . my mother know?"

Rilla was still hanging laundry, but she smiled. "That one's for you."

"Mrs. Stearns—uh, Rilla—" Sonofabitch! He didn't know what to call her. "I'll do right by Jane, I will!"

Yes well, Rilla'd heard all that before. "I'll tell her you came by."

Off balance in that holy-shit-what-do-I-do-now kind of way, Dom said, "Bye, Elva," and nodded to Oak on the ladder and left, forgetting his duffel bag in the driveway. Oak watched for a bit, then finished with the window he'd been holding.

Rilla said, "More pins, girl."

Through the sheets on the line Elva and Rilla could see Dom getting small, getting swallowed up by the tall grass. All that schooling, grooming for the priesthood, the illustrious career meant to stretch out in front of him.

"Poor bastard. Look at him. His life is ruined." It would be Rilla's only judgement.

But Elva thought he looked relieved.

— — —

Elva figured it would turn out like this. Jane would never say boo to Dom about what Gil did, probably because she was worried about what they'd do to each other. Maybe she even felt responsible for what had happened. If she was going to say something, she'd have done it by now, but after she got back from Indian Brook, she and Dom were inseparable, and there was no way Dom, if he knew, could act as if what happened didn't happen. Or so Elva reasoned.

Dom and Jane would get hitched, race off to Sydney, maybe even Halifax. She'd miss Jane dreadfully, maybe even get sick over it like those richy-rich girls on the radio dramas, but a Demerett Bridge without Jane and Dom might be the sort of place Gil would stay in, and then there was all that time she'd have alone with Rilla. So who gave a shit if Jeanine Barthélemy, who apparently was still in the dark over Dom's fall from grace, got pissy over her son going straight to hell? Elva didn't care for her anyhow and thought that Rilla, in her own way, would echo Jane, Haw haw. Maybe her mother might even consider sending Elva to school.

Oak, Elva knew, shared her feelings.

"She'll be leaving," he said in regards to Jane. But then he had to say, which ruined it all, "And when she goes, so will Gil. Should've been gone weeks ago, weeks ago."

The September day was swept away with heavy skies streaked with dull grey, dry, bitter winds and larches yellowing too early. Usually after Dom had spent an evening visiting with Jane, they'd make their goodbyes on the front porch, which could take forever with all the I-miss-you-already's and kiss-kiss-kiss-I-love-you stuff. Elva didn't know for sure, but she guessed there was cooing about baby names and where they'd go and the piano the house in Sydney would have although Jane had no inclination to learn how to play. On this evening, Dom came through the back way into the kitchen where Elva was sitting alone at the kitchen table, swinging her feet back and forth, eating a sandwich of toast and cheese.

"Where's your mother?" he asked, and something was definitely wrong. Wrong in the angry-want-to-kick-something kind of way.

"Indian Brook."

With two men around the house, Rilla figured it was okay to go, although Elva didn't know where Oak was. Hadn't seen him all day.

"Damn. When she gets back, tell her Jane won't marry me."

Elva just blinked.

"Look, is there something going on that she won't tell? Did something happen while I was away?"

Elva slowly shook her head.

"And why won't Gil come over here any more? He's always got some excuse."

Just a shrug this time.

"Fuck." And he left.

Elva sat quietly at the big table, still nibbling her toast and cheese even though her stomach started to flip-flop. Was the truth coming out? Could be just a spat. Lord knows, Jane wasn't the easiest person to love. But why ask about Gil? A door slammed overhead and the hum of the light bulb in the kitchen seemed very loud. Jane won't marry me. Not, I won't marry Jane, or, We can't get married, or, My mother forbids me to marry Jane, but Jane won't marry me.

How could that be? wondered Elva. It's what Jane wanted, didn't she? If Jane didn't marry Dom, that ruined everything—well, if nothing more than the fantasy that Gil might one day be hers. And wasn't that just like Jane! To not even give Elva that. Why in heaven not go away and be happy? Forget about Gil.

Maybe she can't.

What to do? What would Jane do? Jane would have pulled the plug! That's when it occurred to Elva that maybe Jane had been right after all about the sandpiper. Maybe you can't see what needs to be done sometimes, because your heart's right up in your face and you can't even breathe when that happens, let alone make sense of what's good for you and what's bad.

It was right to let that poor bird go. It's right to do it for someone when they can't. And I can do that for Jane. I can tell Dom what Gil did.

The revelation filled Elva with such conviction,

such clarity of purpose, she could only wonder why she hadn't thought of it before. The truth, Elva believed, would help Dom understand Jane's reluctance. However painful the catharsis might be, at some point it would bring peace.

There was shrieking along the shore where the high winds hit the beachhead and roared over the dunes. Not the best of nights for good-deed doing. Elva was glad she'd taken Jane's oilskin, the wind being cold as she stumbled through fields of brown grass drooping heavily, crunching underfoot. The long shadows of evening were giving way to blue, to grey, to black, making short work of a girl's courage. Elva was sure she'd catch up with Dom before he got too far, he hadn't left all that much before her, but damn it, she hadn't thought to bring a lantern.

She was losing her way. Being swallowed. Those old rotten limbs on the dead elm by the Barthélemy farm were creaking something fierce.

"Jane?"

Quiet but sure, he'd startled her. Too dark to see him sitting on the fence lining their road. Dom waiting there, hoping Jane had come to her senses? All Elva could tell was that he was coming towards her.

Frightened, shivering, anxious to get it out and get it over with, Elva did not give him a chance to speak as she nervously garbled out what had happened between Jane and Gil at Ipswich Abbey, even the whole lurid tale of Gil's rent-boy past. Elva had a head of steam going and there was no stopping. So she had broken not only a promise to Jane but a confidence from Oak. Oh well. She hoped that telling Dom about the last five years of his brother's life would soften any retribution. It was only when she paused to catch her breath that she felt something brush her feet and heard the swish of Major's tail against grass.

Gil grabbed her arms, shaking her, squeezing so tightly she felt her bones would pop.

"You're hurting me!"

"How do you know this?"

"Oak told me and, well, there's a secret space from my room to yours—"

"You *saw* us?"

"I know about you and Oak. It's not your fault, you're just trying to prove you're a real man like Dom. But that's okay."

No, far from it. No watcher likes to be watched, and what she could not see in the dark was the transformation in Gil that had withdrawn him from Oak. Running away from himself is what Gil did, and this time it left him marooned between wanting to be Dom and being mad. Elva had upset an uneasy truce.

Gil's grasp tightened. "I could break your fucking neck right now."

Major barked and jumped, like maybe it was play time. Elva felt Gil's hot words as close as a kiss.

"Don't!"

Something in him responded. He dropped her to the ground, staggering away from her.

"I . . . I just wanted to help."

"By telling Dom that I . . . about Jane and me? Jesus Christ, Elva! Do you hate me that much?"

No! No, it's not that way!

"You stupid kid! Dom'll kill me, or Jane, or both of us when he finds out."

Elva scrambled for words, trying to undo damage she hadn't foreseen.

"Not Dom, he's your brother."

He shook her. "Where's Oak?"

Elva said she didn't know, but just who had Gil been sitting in the dark for, hoping to meet?

"Damn! I've got to sort this out," he said quickly, distracted, aloud to himself.

Then —

"Your ol' man's truck. Let's go!"

WHERE WAS THE RAIN? It always rained when the wind blew from the east. Loud, full of spray and sand from the beach, whipping the air with curling, dead leaves—but no rain. Jane used to tease Elva that wind like this could suck out your breath and you'd die of a dry drowning. Right there, plain as day, in the middle of the world.

Elva flew along, dragged by Gil, on the tips of her toes until she tripped in the gravel of the driveway. Get up, get up, he said until she begged, Wait!

"How could you say that I hurt her that I forced her, where's your mother, Elva, how could you even think such things?"

Elva said Rilla wasn't home but stopped herself short of saying she was at her auntie's.

"It wasn't that way, no, Jesus fucking Christ, Elva! I'd never! Not that way, it's not what you think."

"What are you doing?"

He said, "Shut up, Elva," and tossed a handful of stones against the second-storey window of the room he once shared with Oak. No light. Nothing.

"Told you, he's not here."

"Where, damn you?"

"Haven't seen him all day. Sometimes he walks, a long way. I don't know where." *It's because of you that he does.*

He hated the way her voice was quivering, hated that she knew so much about him.

"Fuck!" He looked at the shed and said, "C'mon." Major followed, ears pinned, sensing no fun in this. Elva and Gil struggled to unhinge the wooden doors.

"Christ!"

The wind was too strong. They kept blowing shut. Gil took them in the side door, shutting out the wailing but not the wash-wash-wash of shrubs against the back windows. Gil, Elva and the dog, panting.

"Get in!"

"Where are we going?"

Gil crawled under the steering wheel of the old Ford and worked a few wires together. The truck rumbled and sputtered. Smoke, blue and oily, rose up around them. It stank. Slowly, without lights, he eased out of the shed. Those damned doors banged loudly against the truck, banging back against the sides of the shed, swinging back and shattering one of the headlights.

"Gil, you're scaring me!"

"Shut up, Elva!"

Major barked and they were free of the shed. Elva pushed against her door and before Gil tore out of the driveway, she jumped out of the truck. So too the dog.

"Jesus Christ!"

Gil was faster and before she could even think to scream, they rolled onto the grass, his hand thrust over her mouth.

"Elva, don't fight me!" Gil pushed her back into the truck. "Get in, boy." Major licked her face. The house remained dark. Gil thumped his hands roughly against the steering wheel.

"Don't try that again."

Gil turned the Ford, gears grinding, spitting up gravel, lopsidedly lit with only one headlight, onto the road and headed north past the ponds and the black sentinels of the foundry chimney stacks.

"What are we doing?" Elva asked.

The dog looked as well as if to add, Yes, Master, just what are we doing?

"Going to see Big Head."

"Oh, Gil, I don't like going there!"

"Too bad! You shouldn't have shot your fucking mouth off."

"I won't say anything more. I promise."

"You're not out of my sight until I figure what to do."

She looked at the dark road ahead, barely lit by the remaining light.

"How come you're going there?"

"Gotta get out of here."

"Why not take the bus?"

"Because, Elva, I've done things, remember. I gotta disappear!"

Sprucelike shadows tossed against a starless sky, canopied the winding road. They did not speak. Major sat up expectantly between them. Elva huddled against the door, watching Gil, his face set.

"Maybe Big Head and Squirrel Boy can give me work, get me on a boat to Newfoundland. Get to England from there. Forget about all this."

England! Kingly castles and lawns of green carpet where everyone walked around with a crown, but Elva wasn't thinking about that now.

"Yeah, I know, Elva, why would they help me after the *Meghan Rose*, eh? I'll tell ya, strangest thing, all what folks say about me? Well, right after the accident Big

Head takes me aside and says he didn't hold no grudge against me. Could've happened to anyone, he said. Maybe he'll remember saying that now."

Rilla wouldn't like this, not one bit.

Major settled in for the bumpy ride. Elva felt her eyes get tired as she kept trying to make out things on the side of the road. Raven River, a crossroad with a scattering of houses around a steep pitched Lutheran church set back from the highway, came and went.

A mile or so past the crossroad, Gil pulled onto an S-curved lane and followed it up to the clearing. Jesus, Gil swore as he steered the obstacle course of timber, trusses and piles of finishing stone. There were lights in the ruin.

"C'mon."

"I don't like going in there, Gil."

He jumped out of the truck and pulled Elva with him, Major having to two-step. "Stay, boy," Gil said.

The plank bridge groaned, but weeks of dry weather had left a gully of cracked clay and no mosquitoes. Gil held Elva tightly with one hand, hammered the door with the other. He'd have to repeat it before they heard hurried steps on the other side, like a big mouse, Elva thought.

"Who's there?"

"Gil Barthélemy. I know it's late but I have to see Big Head. Please."

Oh, and the hurried steps went away. Then they came back. Then a blinding square of light. Squirrel

Boy, full in the hips, thin in the neck, with a shock of red hair around a spotted bald crown and head to toe in soupy green Dominion army surplus, shifted from boot to boot like something was wrong with one of his legs. Look who's here, what to do, what to do, Squirrel Boy said, before Gil forced Elva inside.

"Is he here?" asked Gil.

Squirrel Boy was too surprised by the likes of Elva showing up to say anything, to even nod how-do. Elva gazed at the gallery of ancient tits under the languid and haughty gaze of corseted beauties. Air, stinky of the inside of a bait jar, the kind full of worms that Gil used to bring around and tease Jane with when they were little. And the nets. Mosquito nets over everything. A vast indoor three-ring circus, weighted down by years of damp dust and lit by hissing oil lanterns circled by moths.

"Guillaume Barthélemy."

They followed the greeting that sounded like a command into the great room and to the glow from the fire in the monumental hearth. Elva accidentally brushed against the net-cave. It rained a shower of dust.

No, no, no touch, fussed Squirrel boy.

"Nets." From years of trying to sound Canadian, the now only lightly German-accented nasal voice boomed from the fireside chair in the corner. It resonated within Elva. "Bugs here'll cut you to pieces without them."

Big Head was a behemoth of a man, best described as overflowing, fleshy wet folds absorbing his neck, sliding onto his shoulders. Eyes too close together, prominent nose under which a much-preened moustache was pampered and waxed up with a flourish. And, like the Boy, turned out in army fatigues, but with an automatic pistol tucked into his overstretched belt.

"The very last person I'd expect to see, Guillaume. And who's this? You're that washwoman's girl, aren't you?" A cindery glow rose up from Big Head's waist, and as he paused to inhale, the cigarette lit up his face. Creepy. Didn't offer a hand to shake or nothing. "Something for our guests." He gestured to Squirrel Boy, who bobbed and limped out.

Fool got his leg bit and now it's infected, the big man explained. "It'll have to come off. Like to watch?"

Elva shook her head wildly, believing he'd do it right now.

"Oh sit, girl."

Elva did, across from Big Head, but the chair was old and high and her feet didn't touch the floor. The arms were sticky to the touch and she hoped that Gil would hurry and finish here so they could go home where she vowed never to open her mouth again.

"Heard you were back in these parts. From an old associate of ours. Bryant Slaunwhite. Understand you went to work for him when you left here."

Gil tried to betray nothing. "You heard from Bryant?"

"Oh, he was here. Dropped by in the spring. Offered us a little business. I understand he was on his way to New York to see some kind of specialist. Medical condition. Didn't say. Did you know he's taken to wearing a scarf?"

Gil managed, "Really?"

"Asked us to look you up and pass on his regards." Big Head tapped his cigarette. Ashes right on the floor. "Sorry 'bout that. Meant to, but with one thing or another, we never got around to it. Keeping America's spirits up, well, it's a full-time job these days. Been in and out of here, most of the summer. Looks like you've saved us tracking you down."

Squirrel Boy came back with a tray of steaming mugs and a plate of what looked like hardtack. He offered a biscuit to Elva, and Big Head gestured for her to eat, but it was too hard.

"I was hoping, wondering, if you'd get me work. For two. Anything. As long as it's out of province."

Big Head cast a glance at Elva.

"You haven't got this young lady in trouble, have you? She hardly seems your type."

"No!"

And Squirrel Boy laughed.

"Not her. A friend of mine."

"Doesn't want anyone to know. Secret?" said Squirrel Boy.

"Yes."

"Are you in trouble, Guillaume?"

"Just don't want anyone to know where I'm heading." Sit, was the gesture. Gil remained standing. "You did say after, well after you know, that if I needed help—"

"Yes, yes." Big Head waved a biscuit elegantly. "Felt bad about that business with the *Meghan Rose,* you being just a boy and all. Awful. But then you up and left us."

"I couldn't stay."

"No, you couldn't."

"Drink your cocoa," Squirrel Boy said, quietly interrupting the behemoth.

The giant ripped out his pistol and fired, blowing the mug and the table to pieces. Elva screamed, but caught most of it behind her hands. They could hear Major barking distantly in the truck.

"It always tastes like goat piss." Big Head laughed, tucking his pistol back into his belt. "Of course I'll help you, Guillaume. We're all friends here, right? I've got the *Nellie J. Banks* sailing for Canso tomorrow night. Could use your help with our American customers. You and Oak be on it."

Squirrel Boy offered Elva more cocoa.

The single headlight was fading. Major had finally settled down and was curled on the seat beside Elva. Gil drove back to Demerett Bridge in silence, Elva washing under waves of sleep, her head rolling against the seat, but always being knocked back awake.

"Rilla will be worried." Now that Gil had things sorted, he sounded conciliatory, maybe even sorry.

Damn! Roadkill, glowing pulpy red in the head-light, forced Gil to swerve.

Elva wasn't forgiving just yet. She might get all loose-lipped then, and she sure didn't want him to know that Rilla was away for a few days and Jane was home alone. He'd want to see her.

"Christ, Elva, don't you look at me like that. I shouldn't have done this to you. I'm sorry, but don't you see, I had to bring you. I knew they'd done business with Bryant, was afraid they might not help me, maybe worse. Figured nothing would happen to me if you were there. I used you, Elva. I fucking used you. Some man I've turned out to be."

She always dreamed she'd hear someone say, I love you, or even, I came to love you. And perhaps in some way, on some level, Gil cared for her—but not love, not really. Guess she always knew, deep down. The Janes of the world and movie stars got that. Still, Elva cared enough, and always would, to feel sorry for him.

"You are a man, 'cause Jane's baby might be yours."

Another dead animal on the road and Gil turned sharply. "Jesus!" Elva was thrown against the door. "What?"

"I think that's why she won't marry Dom."

Gil stopped the Ford, the headlight cutting a yellow cone into the night. The Major was growling.

"No! That can't be, can it?"

Elva nodded, starting to think she shouldn't have said anything.

"I've got to find Oak. I don't know what to do. Got to think. And this all arranged. I've got us a way out of here. It went so easy, didn't it? Gotta settle things with Oak. I have to see Jane."

Oak. Oak. Yes, the accent. The voice! Now she knew where she'd heard it.

"Gil, Big Head and Squirrel Boy! They were there that night Oak gotten beaten up! It was them!"

"You're crazy."

"No, I'm not. He said something about, I know, a love tap! Yeah, a love tap. It was Mr. Big Head."

It had been easy. Stupid and easy. Gil, desperate for an out, missed all the innuendoes, all the clues, charged away, like taking an oar to Bryant. No thought, no plan. Big Head and Squirrel Boy weren't even trying to hide being in cahoots with the smuggler. Didn't have to. There were plenty of ways for Bryant to get even.

Major was barking.

Gil saw it first from the truck window, stared hard and went dead quiet. He stepped out slowly, his jacket constricting in the wind.

"Don't you move," he said, like his words were pieced together from different people.

The flap of white flesh, the glint of the silver watch. Not just another groundhog or porcupine crushed under the wheels of a truck. Not this time. Elva saw it. Saw him. Left out like garbage, for all to see.

The cab began to shake. The convulsions were hers: body reacting before brain.

THE FORD SPRAYED the driveway with gravel.

Jesus, Elva, Gil was saying, I never said Oak's name, but Big Head knew, I never said Oak, but he did, don't you see, Bryant's found us, Bryant did this because of me.

The door to the truck opened and Elva surfaced into a low wind and blinking stars through scudding clouds. She stumbled up the porch and something pushed her through the screen door and into the hall.

Am I home?

Gil was saying, You're home now, Elva.

Everything is going back and forth. Don't you see?

No answer from Gil. Just the infrequent moon carpeting the way to the kitchen.

It was where he'd left it. Oak's trinket box on the kitchen table full of watch bits and tools waiting for him to walk in and resume his tinkering. She couldn't stop looking.

Don't, Elva, and Gil pulled her away.

Who did that to Oak?

Gil was saying, What to tell Jane?

Felt like someone had added to the staircase. Why else would it take so long to get to the top, every step sending hot pincers through Elva's head?

She'll feel bad now that she burnt his leg with tea and didn't say sorry. Gil? My hands don't grip the railing. She was sure she added, Gil they don't work, but he didn't pay her any mind. *And my feet don't move.*

Gil was saying, Hurry.

You're still afraid, aren't you?

Peek-a-boo went the moon across the floor of her room from the three tall, thin, rectangular windows fronting the house. Curtains by the open casements billowed around the woman waiting in the chair.

You're not Jane. Where's Jane?

Maman? Gil started to close the windows. Why are you here?

I'm in a dream too, don't you know? Elva touched the woman's face.

Don't do that, Jeanine said.

The palms of the woman's hands were facing up, waiting for the nails. Why not crucify her? What a show that'd be. Jeanine'd like that, but not upside down like Saint Peter. Oh no. Her husband, her son, everything of worth, gone. After what she's been through, she deserves to go just like Jesus. Thorns and all.

Where's your mother, girl, she not here with you? None of this would have happened had your mother been home. A girl like that Jane needs her mother.

Maman, Gil asked, where's Jane?

What's the matter with this girl, why don't she speak?

I am speaking, can't you hear me?

Maman, what have you done to Jane? The bed, oh God, the bed, Maman, what have you done?

Gil, why are you hurting your mother like that?

Nothing, said Jeanine. I came to talk to her, only talk. Bitch got my boy's head all confused, take him away from me, from God. He was going to run away. No, I wouldn't have that! Had to. Her and that baby. Domenique thinking it's his!

Gil, the bed? There's so much blood.

Maman, what have you done to Jane?

She's crazy, that girl, look at her, don't she speak?

I don't like dreams where no one can hear me.

Where the fuck is Jane?

Don't shout at me! I came here to help your brother see sense, good and proper.

Dom was here?

Followed him here, replied Gil's mother, after he finished telling me about that girl and the baby. I didn't do nothing to that girl. She was crazy mad when I got here. Kept going on and on about it not being Domenique's. See? I says to Domenique. It's not yours, even though my boy kept saying, shut up Jane you shut up Jane that's my child so you just shut up about that. Tried to talk reason to her, I did. Look, ten dollars! Tried to give her ten dollars to go away, but she wouldn't. It's all the money we have. Just hits herself in the belly like a crazy woman, over and over. She's losing that baby. Wouldn't let me help her.

Maman, for Christ's sake, where's Jane?

I won't have to say anything about Oak now, will I, Gil?

He took her, said Jeanine. Took her away from here!

Where, Maman, where?

Said he'd take her to Halifax like she always wanted, but they won't get far. Needs a doctor, she's poorly. God's blessing if she loses that bastard.

I'm dizzy, Gil. Why is everyone talking fast?

Gil, look at that girl, look at her, she's mad too. Whole crazy family's mad!

Maman, tell me he's not out there tonight with Jane, Jesus Christ, not tonight!

He's got a gun. That slut made him take it, worried because the police can't control the strikers and I said, if you take her out of here, you shoot her! Leave me, leave God, you shoot her like a dog! Hear me, you shoot her and if you go, you break my heart, so shoot yourself too! Rot with your pappa in hell, Domenique, because that's where God'll send you if you go against Him. Send his own pappa to hell for her, he did.

That's Amos's gun. Must have taken it from his room. No one's been in there since . . . Rilla says don't go in there 'cause it still smells of his lemon aftershave and there's a glass by the bed with dried milk in the bottom. Jane did the milk. Not me. I couldn't do the milk.

What's wrong with that Elva girl, Guillaume?

Nothing.

You gotta go out there for your brother.

Leave Elva? No, I can't leave Elva. Not after, well, I just can't leave her.

You find your brother and bring him home. I don't care about that girl. Most likely dead now, bleeding, and good riddance.

I know, Maman, but you go home, you can't stay here.

Why'd Jane not wait to say goodbye to me? Jane should have said, kiss me, because Jane would have wanted to kiss me goodbye, wouldn't she? She's my sister. She'd be wrapped in blankets, in Dom's arms. There'd be tears. Jane, she gets to feel things. Real things. Not me. Dom, he'd kneel so I could hug her.

That one there be okay? asked Jeanine. What's she see out that window?

Elva'll be okay, Maman.

Did he find you?

Who, Maman?

That friend of yours, the tall one, comes to the farm today, says he had something he needed to say.

His name was Oak. Gil, tell her his name was Oak.

I said I don't know where you be and he goes away. Did he find you?

Yes, Maman, I found him.

Elva, will you be all right here on your own? Elva, are you okay, I'll fix this, you'll see, why don't you say something, Elva, why?

I'm not saying anything because I'm trying to wake up and Jane will be in bed beside me and there'll be eggs in butter, smelling good, and Oak will be washing up outside the summer kitchen and . . . you'll hear me . . .

A narrow staircase at the end of the hall, its door next to what had been Gil's and Oak's room, led to the roof. Elva hesitated. What if he's there? But no ghost of Amos—sitting among his beloved stacks of newspaper, saying, Bitch, I know about the milk—was in the attic that night. She crawled to the ladder over the yellowing, damp piles Amos was too miserly to throw out, to the ladder opening onto the widow's walk. The joists underneath creaked.

Dawn was still distant when she emerged onto the roof, but there! There was the foamy tipped crescent of beach all pearly in the windy night, the flickering lights of Demerett Bridge, the nothingness that was Ostrea Lake. The Abbey.

Elva sat against the wind, bracing up here, burying her face between her knees, that sour, wormy stink from that horrible German house still crawling out of her clothes. She had to get rid of it, and she pulled her dress over her head and flung it over the railing of the widow's walk.

Goodbye, Jane. Goodbye, Oak.

Elva, her eyes heavy, shivering in her underclothes, traced her finger over her lips. She'd be safe now until Rilla got home. She'd not be awake long enough to see orange and yellow jagged edges eat across the island, the Abbey, and the dawn.

ELVA TWOHIG WAS MUTE from the moment she saw that boy's cut-up remains strewn across the highway, and would remain so for the rest of her life.

It would be days before anyone noticed.

Rilla had been delayed getting back to Demerett Bridge. Her bus from Indian Brook had been detained by the RCMP on the highway while a group of official-looking men with hats and badges hovered over something hidden under a tarpaulin in the middle of the road. By her window seat, she happened to see one of the officers hold up a silver watch, attached to a chain. Just as her daughter had known, so too did Rilla.

Not trusting the police and certainly not wanting them poking around murky affairs at Kirchoffer Place, Rilla returned home bent to do the only thing she could, remove all trace of her boarder. If anyone ever came around asking questions about the young man whose last name she never even knew, she'd say he'd stayed briefly and moved on. Didn't know anything more. She did not expect to find a monk in her kitchen, Elva sitting at the table in front of a big cup of tea.

There's been trouble, he explained to her. Hard to say just what happened. There'd been a fire. Dom Barthélemy showed up on the lakeshore of the monastery, barely conscious, having floated there from the Abbey in a canoe.

The young Brother, who clearly didn't view this duty as a fun way of getting out of vespers, went on to say that Dom had been severely burned: face, arms, the left side of his body. He was at the monastery now, refusing to see anyone, even his mother.

Because he's not Dom, Elva said, but by now she had realized that no one could hear her.

Dom did manage to say, the bad news went on, that his brother and Jane are out there. Murder-suicide is

what the Brother told Rilla. With flames still smouldering, no one had been able to get to the Abbey to verify.

Elva had never seen her mother cry, nor would she
now. After they were alone, Rilla sat at the table for a
long time, saying only this: Oak's dead, and, We show
no tears to no one. Then she got up, found a package of
Amos's cigarettes from his things in his room and took
them out onto the back step with a half-empty bottle of
bourbon. She stayed there until dark. When Rilla nodded off, Elva, the screen door creaking behind her, went
out and helped her back into the living room, settling
her mother on the sofa and covering her with a blanket.

Elva then went up to her room and, because of the
still bloody bed, took her pillow and blanket and lay
down on the floor, staring up at the cracks in the ceiling.
The house felt very empty. She did not sleep.

The next morning she watched them dig a grave on the
other side of the tar ponds from her bedroom window.
There was a police car and a truck outside the gates
to the Franciscan monastery. She knew the grave was
for Oak.

Gather up everything, Rilla had said. She meant
Oak's things. When Elva had done that, they put his
few bits of clothing, his leather tool case and the velvet
bag with his watch pieces into his brown striped suitcase and snapped it shut. Rilla didn't say anything
about Elva taking from his room her three pictures that

Oak had admired and including them. Then Rilla took
the suitcase to the ponds and sank it in the tar. Standing
from her dirty task, she watched Elva walking to the
Eye through the tall grass on the other side.

DON'T MIND, Elva thought in regards to her lost voice. Wherever it had gone, it had taken away the images of Oak on that road. She figured it'd be back. In time, she came to think of it gone as a blessing. When she was asked what happened out there, or what about Jane, she'd hear answers in her head. No one else would. The thing about that, not actually saying the words made her not quite feel the pain of Jane being gone, pain at all for that matter. So it was that she was able to lie beside the fresh-turned ground and miss Oak instead of grieve for him.

They'd buried him beside the north stone wall, hidden under a grove of larches and the nearby sound of the fountain. It was private, out of the way, and every fall he'd be covered with a yellow bower. She thought Oak would like that. Elva knew she'd not find any wildflowers this late in the season so she'd brought her writing tablet, one that he'd given her, and sketched out a bouquet. She'd been working on that when she felt tired and thought, close my eyes a few minutes and I'll finish it.

Elva was awakened suddenly by sharp cries and yells. Thousands of glowing fireflies were falling, stinging her arms and legs and face, the afternoon gone dark, the air thick with smoke.

Hurry! Hurry! This way, someone was yelling, the sound of metal gates swinging open. People were running, coughing, calling out names. On the dirt mound beside Elva, the pages of her writing tablet curled up one after the other in flame.

The sizzling came first, then the stench from her burning hair. Elva scrambled to her feet, swatting her head, but the smoke filling her after every sob emptied out more breath. It grew hotter and harder to find air and the voices sounded more distant. She heard a window shatter.

"Elva!"

Then she heard it again.

"Elva! Elva!"

He groaned as he caught her, falling, dragging her against the stone wall for what little protection it afforded. She could not see him clearly, but she could feel his rough skin, heard the tipple of water. That roughness, it was gauze, bandages.

There was another voice now, panicky, rapid, saying Dom what is Elva doing here you have to get out of here now, hurry Dom, hurry! It was John the sexton, arms flapping under the stinging rain.

The brownness of the air was lightening to orange, becoming hotter and thicker, blowing in from all sides.

"For fuck's sake, you have to get out!"

The wounded man wrapped himself around Elva and she heard him say they'd never make it to the gate. He rolled her, the pain pinching an unholy sound from him, placing Elva into the lower bowl of the fountain.

"Are you crazy?" John was shouting. "Get out! Get out!"

"Jesus Christ!" he replied as much from the pain as to try and shut the sexton up. Cupping his hands, he bathed Elva's face and hair.

Thunder rattled somewhere out over the sea and the drops began. Heavy. Plunking drops sounding like pebbles. Then more and faster, until the rain cooled the stinging on Elva's face.

Evening Mail
November 3, 1927

GOD SAVES TOWN

Demerett Bridge, Nova Scotia, was saved yesterday
from a wildfire by what locals insist was nothing
short of a miracle. An eyewitness claims the fire was

stayed when a man called upon the Lord to save a young trapped Mi'kmaq girl.

The conflagration, authorities report, resulted from the flare up of an earlier fire on a small lake island behind the town proper. Wind-fanned flames spread embers across Ostrea Lake into the woods, where unseasonable weather has left conditions extremely dry. Several fires burned out of control along the outer perimeter of the lake, threatening both the town to the northeast and the Maritime Foundry Corporation and a religious order to the south. Several homes and businesses in the community of Raven River west of Demerett Bridge were, however, destroyed.

Demerett Bridge is home to the Maritime Foundry Corporation, which has been in a long and bitter labour dispute with its union.

Citizens of Halifax and Truro were quick to respond to the stricken community with offers of aid and medical assistance. Early reports suggest the province will convene an investigation.

The inquiry began at the end of the month, and the only place large enough to handle the proceedings and the crush of the curious was the Towne Theatre, already doing double duty rehearsing the Christmas pageant due to smoke damage at the parish hall. Each evening the movie screen would have to be restored on the former burlesque stage, taken down in the morning under the bemused but unblinking eyes of the papier-mâché caryatids in each corner, blue-painted tassels hanging from the nipples of their gravity-defying tits. With breaks and adjournments, even the odd fainting spell, the schedules between the two conflicting spectacles overlapped. Often the gallery for the inquiry was filled with high-school girls who made up the retinue of fairies and snow princesses, all lithe and thin, humming their dance numbers and cheerfully waving cigarettes around, careful not to sear each other's wings or the goat for the Baby-Jesus-in-the-Manger sequence.

Rilla wore her new hat, the first piece of brand-new store-bought clothing she'd ever owned. She had purchased it for Jane's funeral. Black felt, round like a cereal bowl, with a purple ribbon. With her daughter laid to rest and it being close to Christmas, Rilla thought nothing of adding a sprig of spruce and a couple of cranberries. No lifetime of mourning for her. A preacher from Preston—part of the sideshow camped out in front of the theatre each day, and backed up by a humming choir swaying like bullrushes—thought her disrespectful of the solemn proceedings and didn't mind saying so.

Alighting from a crucifix-adorned staging as if slow marching up a wedding aisle, the preacher man pointed an accusing finger at the cranberries. Such bold finery meant only one thing, an errant, prideful woman, and there was still time to heel to God's almighty call! The bullrushes in behind were praising the Lord. Those who'd gathered to try to get a seat for the proceedings surged forward. The newsreel cameras started whirring and clicking. Rilla's arms circled Elva as the flashes went off: *poomff! poomff!* Look this way! *Poomff.* Spent bulbs shattering on the pavement.

The delay caused them to miss out on seats in the orchestra, making Rilla forget she'd brought apples for them to eat, and she never wore that damned hat again. They'd have to go up. Rilla said, Follow the angels' wings and saddle shoes to the balcony, where one of them asked Elva to be a luv and light her fag because her nails were still wet with polish. Rilla gently pulled Elva away and they took two seats at the front.

Someone was yelling for quiet and to please take the Christmas pageant goat outside.

They sat by the balcony railing, where Elva rested her chin on her hands and looked down. Almost like a church crowd except that there had been fights to get in and no church that Elva knew smelled like cold cream and pancake makeup. She self-consciously felt for the healing scar on her forehead where her hair had burned. Let it alone, said Rilla.

There was buzzing in the gallery about the just-over strike. Union men, rushing to the buckets, had saved their livelihood from ruin. In turn, the grateful owners of the Maritime Foundry Corporation yielded to demands for higher wages and a shorter work week. Boarders were already returning to Kirchoffer Place.

"Would John Solomon Purvis please step forward," began the day's affairs after a call to order and some official swearing of stuff on Bibles. Rilla had told her daughter that everyone has to tell the truth after swearing, but Elva wasn't clear if the book made you do it or it was something you yourself had to come up with. Might be a bit of a flaw in the whole thing as far as Elva was concerned.

When the elderly man came in, he glanced up and nodded to Rilla. Not like that Jeanine Barthélemy, sitting down there in the same row as the mayor and town council. She never looked at Elva or Rilla again. But Mr. Purvis did. Elva knew him now on account of him being such a kindly man when after the fire he said, Might as well bury them here, place is ruined for anything else. So they did. Elva was glad. Everything black and crunchy didn't seem so hurtful surrounded by all that cool lake water.

He was directed by one of the three men sitting at a long table on the stage, flanked by red-velvet curtains. They all wore dark suits, and the man in the middle, who appeared to be the leader but who never spoke except behind his hand when he leaned sideways to the others, had round glasses and a wooden hammer. It was only an inquiry and not a court with milords, but he'd hammer away just the same.

Mr. Purvis stepped onto the stage aided by a cane more for show than support. He'd told Elva it was called a shillelagh, came all the way from Ireland and if anyone got out of sorts at the proceedings, he'd bop them on the head. She managed her first smile in weeks after that.

His elegant, suited appearance silenced the theatre to hushed whispers. Well, take a good look. This was the crackpot who'd built that oversized playground on the island. The first witness of the day sat at the small table in the corner and folded his hands.

Did he swear to tell the truth? the man on the left was asking.

"Naturally." He gave his name and said he was retired from the Bickford-Ensign Company. "Yes, sir, indeed they do make fuses."

Where was he from?

"Connecticut, where I make my home, but I summer here. I came years ago on vacation. That's how I purchased the land. A hobby of sorts."

So he was, in fact, the owner of the island in Ostrea Lake.

Mr. Purvis nodded.

What could he say of the damage?

"Destroyed completely."

"Where you aware of any machinery stored on the island?"

"From time to time, for the gardens, to build the structures."

"Any petrol?"

"Yes, I believe so. In a shed, by a shed, maybe." He looked around the theatre as if to add, I bet you sons-of-bitches will all come now to see the island.

They thanked Mr. Purvis.

And that was that.

Rilla said, "Sit back, Elva, and pay attention."

Someone with a round silver microphone from the radio station in Halifax was explaining to "Hello out there in Radioland!" that Mr. Purvis had just left the stand. Very silkily he added that the sponsor for this hour was McCaffery's Tooth Powder, for the happiest smiles of your life.

The policeman was next.

He appeared smaller down on the stage than in person. When he sat, he removed his hat and put it on the table beside him. Elva hadn't noticed before that he was balding and he'd shaved off what was left. He looked very nervous.

"You led the investigation of the island after the fire?"

"That's correct, sir."

"What were your findings?"

"The fire started on the island. We found two bodies, sir. On the shore farthest away from town."

There was a gasp in the theatre, although everyone already knew that.

"Were you able to identify them?"

The policeman's head was sweating but he made no move to wipe if off, in case it was rude.

"Yes, sir. Guillaume Barthélemy and the Indian girl, Jane Twohig."

No, it's not Gil, said Elva.

"Anything else?"

"Well, sir." The policeman swallowed like a big lemon jujube had gone down sideways. "She looked as if she'd . . . miscarried."

The official man in the middle had to hammer the table to bring order. Folks weren't used to hearing about dead babies in public like that. The radio man was talking a mile a minute into his microphone.

"All from Demerett Bridge," the policeman added when he could.

Elva wasn't sure if you could say that about the baby considering it hadn't been around long enough to be from anywhere.

"What can you say about the deceased?"

"Well, the Indian girl looked like she was dead before the fire."

"What makes you say that, and remember, constable, there are ladies present."

He said there was no evidence that she'd fought the flames.

"And young Barthélemy?"

No evidence of that either.

"Thank you, constable. Anything else?"

"Well, sir, it appears Guillaume Barthélemy—"

"Yes?"

"We think he started the fire."

Jeanine was shaking her head, shouting at the men behind the table, but Elva couldn't hear what because everyone else was shouting too.

Bang! Bang! Bang!

"Continue."

"By accident. There was a gun, sir."

"Had it been used?"

"Yes, sir. On himself."

That caused another uproar, and Elva leaned back into Rilla's arms. *It's not Gil.*

"The bullet, begging your pardon," continued the policeman, finally having no choice but to wipe off his head, "after it passed through Barthélemy, must have hit the gas can nearby. That how the fire started."

Someone with a weak stomach ran up the aisle and out the door, letting in the sounds of the Preston choir and the growing crowd getting nearer my God to thee.

"Were you able to determine who owned the gun?"

"Yes, sir. Amos Stearns. Deceased. The Indian girl's mother worked for him."

Worked, indeed. That brought laughter. Elva squeezed Rilla's hand.

The pause in the proceedings made the fairies and snow princesses restless, stamping their saddle shoes, making Elva pukey from their cigarettes.

"Now they're bringing in the next witness," the radio man was saying in a church voice as the doors in back opened and people craned for a glimpse. "This, folks, is the man everyone is here to see. The very man who saved that young girl's life!" Radio man's last word came out kind of breathless.

The witness was on a bed carried by four Franciscans in coarse robes and sandals, even though it was nigh December. Only his head stuck out from under the blankets and his face was completely bandaged. A nurse with a hat that curled at its edges carried a bottle, hooked to a pole, hooked to him. She smiled at the policeman who now stood off to the side. The nurse was part of the medical contingent that came from Halifax and as far away as Saint John, turning the monastery into a field hospital to deal with all the cases of smoke inhalation and burns.

"They're placing him centre stage."

There was no point in hammering the table until everyone had resumed sitting. They'd all ignore it anyhow.

"Your name, sir? We must have your name for the proceedings."

He would not be able to be heard, so one of the Franciscans hovered over the mummy-man and acted as a megaphone.

"He says, Domenique Barthélemy."

Liar!

"This inquiry thanks you, Mr. Barthélemy, for being here. We offer condolences and we'll be brief, under the circumstances. Now what can you tell us about the night of the fire?"

Dom's aide bent low and listened. Everyone in the movie theatre did likewise. Someone sniffled. Elva thought it sounded like a Jeanine Barthélemy sniffle. Father Cértain was beside her and offered a hand-kerchief.

When Dom was finished the monk nodded, stood, folded his hands and addressed the panel.

"Domenique Barthélemy, brother to the deceased, says the Indian Twohig asked him to take her to the island to hide the shame of her illegitimate child. They were met and challenged by Guillaume Barthélemy. Domenique Barthélemy says his brother was distraught over the Indian Twohig's condition for which he claimed responsibility. Domenique Barthélemy says he tried to convince his brother to return home. He would not. During an altercation between the two men, the Indian Twohig succumbed to the effects of a miscarriage."

Rilla had Elva's hand clutched in hers, slowly squeezing tightly until Elva was sure her mother was thinking, Why couldn't it have been you?

"Guillaume Barthélemy then shot himself with a gun the Indian Twohig had given to Domenique Barthélemy for her protection, the bullet continuing on into a can of gasoline. Domenique Barthélemy received these extensive injuries when he tried to contain the blaze."

Was that everything?

"That is the evidence."

While everyone else debated what they'd heard, and the man with the microphone gave his listeners an idea of how many bandages wrapped Dom's face, the three men at the table conferred behind the hands of the man in the middle.

"Order, please! This inquiry thanks Domenique Barthélemy and wishes no further questions for this witness."

The entourage, and nurse, packed Dom up and carried him out of the theatre. Jeanine Barthélemy had to be restrained by Father Cértain.

"Why doesn't he want to see me, his own mother?" she kept saying. "Why?"

Outside, the crowd broke off being nearer to God and silently cleared a swathe. Men removed their hats. Dom had refused to be sent to Halifax for treatment, and the monastery had become his hospital, then his home. He would rarely be seen again outside of its walls.

John Ingram was the last witness to be called. It was getting close up in the balcony, feathers were falling out, and the projectionist was bitchin' that he had *The Road to Mandalay* with Lon Chaney waiting in the wings.

John made his way to the witness table, his hands clasped together as if in prayer, eyes lifted to the theatre ceiling, which would have to pass for heaven. He had no suit coat or Sunday tie, but his shirt was buttoned to the neck and he looked well scrubbed.

Poomff! Poomff! The press loved him. The photographer from the Halifax paper missed John's entrance and could he please walk across the stage again. The inquiry, and John, accommodated the request, and when he was finally seated John was asked what he knew about the fire.

With his hands pressed together, shaking them skyward, he said, "We were saved by the tears of—"

He couldn't say, John being one of those folks who's too Catholic to say Jesus unless they've accidentally whacked the crap out of a finger. Then it's usually accompanied by fuckin' or jumpin' or both. So he just looked humble, knowing that everyone could tell he'd been touched by the nameless one. Hollywood's flickering black-and-white images emoting on the movie screen had nothing on this guy.

"It's a miracle, I tell you! I saw it with my own eyes! A miracle! Domenique Barthélemy called on the Lord and it rained right then, and saved Demerett Bridge, I swear it before God!"

The less than scientific in the crowd were on their feet shouting, waving, fainting, Liar! or Praise God! drowning out the hammering from the stage. John's declaration was carried by commotion outside to the preacher, who pushed forward, insisting he be let inside and that no miracle was going to happen without his okay. The man chairing the inquiry from the long table finally took to his feet and, with outstretched arms, begged to be heard. John was not finished. Running to the edge of the stage, he insisted it was all true.

"If you don't believe me, ask her!"

He pointed directly at Elva in the balcony.

"Domenique Barthélemy saved her, us! She's the girl, the girl in the fountain! She knows what happened! She saw him do it!"

"We're out of here," Rilla said, glancing to the doorway.

Wings began to flutter. The angels had other plans. People from outside, spurred on by the head of steam the choir had built up, poured into the theatre, clogging the stairwells to the balcony. Those seated below pushed backwards for a glimpse of Elva, trapping those in the balcony from any exit.

"Bring her down. She must give evidence!"

The angels were swarmed by folks from outside desperate to squeeze in for a seat, breaking their feathered appendages, shoving them out of the way. Rilla, hanging on to Elva, helplessly tried to break through the crowd to the stairs. On the stage, they were banging that stupid wooden mallet and calling for Elva. Some

kindly sorts around Rilla said she couldn't get down
that way, too many people.

"Then hand her over the balcony!"

Over the balcony? Elva clung tightly to her mother.
Rilla's hat was knocked over her eye.

"They want her down below, ma'am. Let's go, little
lady! Won't hurt you a bit. We won't drop you, ha ha."

They had to pry Elva's fingers one by one off her
mother.

Stop them!

Rilla said, "She can't say anything" as they gently
but forcefully took Elva and lifted her over the balcony
to the outstretched arms below.

There you go, they said, Didn't hurt a bit, did it?

One of the men on the stage yelled this was most
irregular.

They passed Elva over heads up to the stage. Whee!

Poomff! Poomff!

It's the half-breed Indian girl some claim witnessed
the miracle, the man behind the microphone was saying
after reminding them for the umpteenth time to brush
their teeth as a terrified Elva sailed overhead. Flashes
and hot bulbs were bouncing from cameras everywhere. They put Elva in the witness chair and thrust a
Bible at her. The lights were blinding and she held it
with the wrong hand. The man in the middle raised his
arms and the theatre finally went silent. Elva looked
like a wee bird up there and even her mother in the

balcony could see her trembling. Outside, whistles were blowing from the police trying to control the restive crowd from spilling into the street. Someone coughed and Rilla said, "She can't speak."

Almost six weeks to the day after the fire, Major came back. Rilla had just left in the truck to make laundry rounds. She no longer went to Raven River. Elva was at the sink washing dishes when she glanced out the window and there he was, sitting pretty-as-you-please in the middle of the driveway.

Elva almost sailed through the screen door and headfirst into the gravel getting to him, and Gil's dog was just as excited to see her. He was limping from a burn that had begun to scab and pus over on his back leg and he was dreadfully thin, but otherwise happy to be back where he considered home.

"Sweet Jesus!" Rilla said when she came back and found Elva sketching the dog on the front porch. After all that had happened, she'd given up on the not swearing thing and hoped the good Lord wouldn't hold it against her on Judgment Day.

Of course he has to stay, Rilla conceded, after what that poor animal had endured, and they could only imagine! She helped Elva put salve on the dog's wound and they fed him in turns until he'd eaten his fill. Elva wanted Major to sleep in her bed that night, but there was no way he'd leave that spot outside Gil and Oak's old room.

Several days later Rilla told Elva the dog needed air and she thought his leg was up to it. No doubt he missed his walks with, well, you know. Elva was glad to get away from Kirchoffer Place. Sometimes it was crowded. Foundry workers were back and Jane and Oak were there when they were not there. Strike over, there was no fear waiting in the fields, only memories, but maybe the dragonflies would scare those off by next summer.

She'd wanted to go to the beach, remembering that Major liked to swim and drink scoopfuls of seawater. How he never got sick, Elva didn't know. Instead he darted across the road and chose a path around the tar ponds. She still had trouble keeping up. Every morning, they took the same route, to the same place.

PART TWO

1970

STUPID FUCKIN' CHRIST, said little Harry Winters—except Harry wasn't little any more. The water he threw at Elva dripped off her face onto the breadbox she was painting.

Another rumour of a miracle in the tabloids had sent Winters to the cathedral for more holy water from the fountain. Surely if the tears of the Lord quelled seizures in some Dartmouth kid whose parents had more than enough to pay for a good doctor, they could make Winters a woman he might bear to touch, eh? Well, no miracle today. Just a disappointed Harry putting an old honey jar in the shape of a teddy bear on the shelf by the window, in case the water did work later on warts.

Elva's husband disappeared for the rest of the day, returning late with a gal he'd sat across from at the bingo hall in Duplak's former emporium. The king of the five-and-dime was long gone, didn't even see out the end of the war, but his store still smelled of pine shavings and overripe fruit. Mrs. La-de-da tried to make a go of it, but after a few years she sold up and vanished into a mysterious place called New Jersey. *Lion's Bingo* was on the nameplate over the door now and, as everyone including Winters knew, legions or bingo halls were better than a bar for hooking up with women, if you weren't too particular about hair like cotton candy or a mouth full of Juicy Fruit.

His bingo marker had run out and that cheap bastard would never buy a new one, not when there was a smiling woman with pink lip gloss and emerald lids who'd lend you one. Not that she was any great shakes. But his old dad used to say, Harry, you've got the dick, they've got the slit. So when she offered Winters her orange marking stick, he winked and she grinned back and he knew he had this one bagged.

"That her?" Her face flushed as Winters pushed her in through the door. They both stank of draft beer, somehow managing to hold each other up. "Poor dear. Don't look like much."

Then she saw the paintings. Wild, vibrant, raw, brilliantly coloured, everywhere, on everything, a maze, a map, astounding.

Winters licked the back of the woman's neck and laughed. "I'll have to charge you two bucks likes I get from the tourists if you look any longer."

With a slap to her ass they started up the narrow stairs to the loft, but the woman stopped halfway.

"Don't you worry. Ol' Noddie's a queer thing." Winters was always considerate to explain how things were, like how his wife's weakening neck and shoulder muscles made her head nod. "She's fucked in the head. Don't speak a word."

In a few minutes, the rhythmic squeal of the bed-springs increased along with, No no no, which of course meant, Yes yes yes! The springing intensified. If you put your hand to the wall you could feel the vibrations. Elva gathered up her jars of colour and cans of brushes and moved her TV tray to the other side of the room. Not that you could get away from it.

Next morning, after Winters left for a few days' fishing, Elva served tea and toast to the bingo girl. Elva always served tea and toast to his girls.

"I love your paintings. I said, I love your paintings. You old cow, what's the matter with you? I said, I, oh, right, you can't talk. Poor thing, I don't know how he manages with her."

I'm not deaf.

When Elva was finally shut of this one, she walked out to the shoulder of the highway. Mrs. Dorey of the next farm over, overlooking where the tar ponds used to be, wanted something of Elva's handiwork for her granddaughter in Alberta. Elva thought an empty tobacco tin covered in yellow and lavender kittens would do nicely. Make sure she pays for it, Winters had said.

Now, much had changed since she had last seen Kirchoffer Place. A sign projecting the opening of another motel in Demerett leaned in the sand nearby. The Bridge part was long gone. Dropped off. Anyway, there hadn't been a bridge in town longer than any cared to remember. Demerett, once home to shore birds, was now a magnet for tourists.

They came in air-conditioned buses with toilets. Imagine. That's why they tore down the old houses like Rilla's and built motels. At night, a thin pink glow stretched across distant hills that had once been brooding with forest. Now they were covered with developments, with patio doors and angel-stone hearths and Kelvinators in the kitchen, marketed with a view of the Abbey.

Easier to get to now with the road. They had to put

it in when they enlarged the island to add a parking lot. So many people wanted to see the star-crossed lovers' graves. And that's just what the sign over the ticket booth said. Afterwards, visitors could take a ride on the Ferris wheel, rent a paddle boat or browse the gift shop selling half-dollar editions of Jane's life that didn't even get the year she was born right.

The biggest change of all, of course, was the cathedral. Like something made on the beach by dripping wet sand into towers, only bigger, much, much bigger. They called it Our Lord of the Tears. Part of it covered over that fountain. She hadn't seen it in years, but Winters said it was pretty much the way it always was, except cleaner and surrounded by lots of gold and walls of crutches and wheelchairs from sickies who'd been given the cure. They had to fill the tar ponds with shale and pave them over for the bus lots. They were mostly full, especially on the anniversary of the miracle.

Yes. That miracle. The idea of it made Elva clap her hands and laugh, something she wasn't caught doing too often.

A chunk of the old Franciscan monastery remained. Winters said it's pretty much empty now. They haven't had to make cheese for over twenty years. Miracles were big business for the Church. At night, there'd be a single light in the upstairs window. The light might have been his. Blessed by God, they say. But Elva knew. Yes, she knew all about him. Damned by God, she'd say. Him

in the lighted room across the parking lot with just a cot,
surely a crucifix; Elva silent in her arthritic body. They
shared this—they were both suffering. He most of all.

At first she painted cows and pigs and Christmas
trees on pieces of tile and linoleum, cats with blue
tongues on kitchen canisters. Winters found he could
sell them to tourists and in summer set up shop outside
the house. But they were just practice. Always in the
back of Elva's mind was painting something magical.
Not larger than life, their lives. Needing a broad canvas,
all she had was her tiny house. And a vision.

Because Jane was right.

Elva was thirty-three in 1947 when Rilla placed the
advertisement in the paper: *Slightly crippled white woman
seeking marriage. Can do light housework. $500. Apply
R. Stearns, Box 315, Kirchoffer Place, Demerett Bridge,
Nova Scotia.*

The dowry came from a Hollywood producer who'd
visited Demerett, paying Rilla for the right to make a
movie about Jane, starring Linda Darnell. But Miss
Darnell decided to do *Forever Amber* and that was the
end of that.

Writing the advert had been difficult. To get the
best rate Rilla had to keep it under twenty-five words.
Demerett had its own eight-page weekly by now, *The
Post & Banner,* so the girl in the newspaper office helped.
Elva knew her mother fudged about the half of her that

wasn't white, technically speaking, and she didn't mind the wording, not that she could read it. Rilla was getting on and Elva's congenital weaknesses were worsening. No doubt about it, the day was coming when she'd need help and Rilla'd be gone. So Elva worked it out, that the bit in the newspaper was Rilla really saying, I love you, girl. There was only one response, Harry Winters.

Rilla said he was, if nothing else, determined, when he arrived half an hour early for his appointment and was shown into Amos's sitting room. Elva waited in one of Rilla's dresses, with refreshments.

"Don't like to give a pass to opportunity," he said, helping himself to another slice of cake with his coffee. Winters had only recently arrived back in town, having been with the army since '39 and, when the war ended, trying his luck down in Halifax. Upon seeing Elva he added, "Don't figure there'll be much competition."

Rilla said of course there were other applicants, so why had he applied?

"Well, see, it's the money. Don't have any trouble telling you that. And in case you hadn't noticed, I'm not exactly Cary Grant. No one's fixin' to tie up at my dock. Five hundred dollars'll get me a right some boat I've an eye on. Maybe a groundfish licence too. Expect I'll do all right."

The honesty was to his credit.

"Ma'am, I know'd her for years and she knows me. I can promise the little lady here a roof, not a grand one like this, but a dry one. And three squares a day. But she'll have to cook." It was, after all, only five hundred dollars.

Rilla wanted to know what assurances she had that he would not put Elva out once money had changed hands.

"I give you my word."

Not good enough.

Elva watched the negotiations dispassionately, first looking at Rilla, then at Winters. She was trying to find something of value, anything, in the man or in the situation, but could only think of begonias.

"Yeah, but you can't expect me to marry her."

An unmarried woman living with a bachelor? What would people think?

Jane would have found that funny, and Elva had to look away in case she laughed.

"I don't expect they'll be thinking anything," Winters said, glancing sideways at Elva.

What if the five hundred came with the expectation that this house was to follow, upon Rilla's death?

Winters whistled. Like they say, that was a horse of a different colour. A right big horse. Interested, sure, but he had to see the whole place before he agreed.

Elva and Winters were married quickly and quietly at the new brick town hall with a working clock. Quietly, because people in Demerett had become rather protective of Elva. At least, about the *idea* of Elva. Sort of like the Virgin Mary. No one wanted to think that the

girl in the fountain did anything after the big event but
kneel and pray. Marriage, with all its sweating and
groaning under the sheets on a Saturday night, was tar-
nish on silver plate. They needn't have worried.

Without a honeymoon they moved to the one-room-
with-loft house built by, and for, a bachelor with few
needs. Winters insisted they make do. Elva's first lesson
in her married life: her husband was tight. Why waste
money on something bigger when they had that fine
house coming their way?

If things had gone according to plan three years later
when Rilla died, Elva might never have conceived her
masterwork, continuing, rather, to paint bits and pieces,
odds 'n' ends. Elva'd never have defiled the walls in
Rilla's house with her paintings. It would have been like
painting over Jane and Oak.

But the house did not come to Elva and Winters
after Rilla died on that June day, when Barry Daryl
Bedell (he insisted upon giving his full name in the
police report) said it had scared the bejesus out of him.

The boy was riding his bike past Kirchoffer Place,
coming down from shooting squirrels with his BB gun
in the hills and, No, he didn't get none, the windows just
exploded. The one over the front porch and that one,
next to it. Glass everywhere, stuff coming out like the
house was barfing.

None of that now, his mom said. Tell the officer true

what happened and mind your mouth. But Barry was only eight and that's what it looked like to him.

When the policeman drove Barry and his mom home, they stopped first to explain everything to Elva and Winters. They began by saying they had no idea how many tons of paper had actually been stored in the house. What they did know was that the floor collapsed, flushing all that paper down onto Rilla reading in her bed, washing it and her out the front upstairs windows. It took hours of digging to find her.

Amos couldn't throw a newspaper out after he'd read it on account of the money spent, so he piled them against the walls in the attic. And don't anyone try and take one, he'd say, for he claimed to know where every single day for the last twenty-five years was. Probably did, too.

Learning had come hard to Rilla. Circumstances had decreed reading a luxury, and any spare time Rilla had was usually spent with both her hands elbow deep in hot sudsy water. Amos didn't think a native woman had the brains for it, so she never even looked at a newspaper if he was near, not if she didn't want a slap to the side of the head. Then Amos was dead and Jane was dead and there was a living for her and Elva to be made. The strike was over and the boarding house was once again full. Rilla unexpectedly found herself an entrepreneur, and the papers, never stopped, kept coming. She figured it was in her best interests to understand what the world had to say. Or at least, what the papers thought she should know. She began to read in earnest, sounding out letters, childlike, reading aloud but with quiet determination.

Such a hard-won accomplishment bestowed upon the papers an almost reverential quality, every word symbolic. Rilla circled the name Jane found anywhere inside, like maybe they were coded messages from beyond. The weight on the attic floor continued to grow.

Elva wanted to ask if Rilla had suffered, but of course she couldn't. The policeman handed over some newsprint found in her mother's hand, saying it might mean something to her kin. Elva couldn't read it, so the officer told her the *Evening Mail* article was a piece about a man in Halifax who'd had a checkered past, smuggling during the glory days of Prohibition. Bryant Slaunwhite was now a member of the Kiwanis Club, supported the Boy Scouts and ran a gardening store called Topiary on Young Street, in one of the hydro-stone houses built after the explosion in '17. He was being feted for having just published his memoirs, *High Seas Running,* where among many of his exploits, he recounted doing business with a pair of German-Canadians who'd drugged their crew with coffee laced with laudanum and scuttled their schooner, using the insurance money to finance a bootleg operation.

What condition is the house in now? Winters demanded, adding that it was his, well, his wife's inheritance and did anyone think he could successfully sue the newspapers for the damage? And for his mother-in-law's death, of course.

The last word went to Barry, who was transfixed by the gnomey-looking woman with a half-painted breadbox in her lap and a smear of ochre on the side of her nose.

"It looked like snow, all them papers coming out of the windows and flying about," he said. "Just like winter."

Snow in June.

That's enough, corrected Mom. "Show a little respect. That crazy lady's just lost her mother."

Inside Elva's house for most of the 1960s, as American draft dodgers opened gift shops on Commercial Street and the foundry closed because it was cheaper to pay steelworkers in pesos, it remained that summer of 1927. Admittedly, the project had long periods of delay. Ill health was the more vexing problem; chronic rheumatoid arthritis often left Elva exhausted and unable to work.

Every morning when she was well enough, she'd stoke the fire, and after a breakfast of oatcakes and mint tea, she'd settle herself in the corner underneath the potted geraniums along the windowsill, a rainbow of petals sure to dust her shoulders. The day's work began with fussing over the TV tray that held her paints, a thickly bubbled kaleidoscope of oily drippings.

During the long winter months when her husband was often away for weeks at a time at whatever fishing/logging/road construction job he could sweet-talk himself into, a boy from Demerett stopped by twice, sometimes three times a week. Anders Hamilton made sure Elva had enough firewood piled inside the back door, brought supplies and what mail there might be. A thick-necked boy not graced with comeliness, he was taciturn at best. Elva didn't mind. Something about his eyes reminded her of Oak. Occasionally her curiosity got the best of her and she'd wondered if Anders ever had a girlfriend, what his mum did, if he could have one wish, what would it be. He only talked to her once. His hockey team had won a regional tournament and he was still pretty flamed about it. Like Elva would know what a shutout was.

So Elva was not completely alone even though her husband's cabin was a few miles outside Demerett. When the roads became snow clogged and she wrapped herself in a felt car blanket against draughts, days passed before she'd see anyone drive by. She liked these times most of all. Surrounded by spring-in-pots, armed with an idea given to her years ago by Oak, Elva conceived her vision as a series of panels, carefully sketching them out on a sheet of plywood, noting every detail before daubing colour to wall, to banister, to stair riser, to stove pipe, to window. Winters hated them. What's the fucking point about decoration? is what he wanted to know.

He wanted her to paint only what he could sell. But each time he returned home after a lengthy absence, another section of house had been storied.

Seeing her gaily painted cottage door and window, folks on the way to the cathedral would stop, sometimes for a picture. By the end of the sixties, tourists were driving from as far as Boston just to see her. Elva's painted squares of linoleum, her breadbox and clay flowerpots garnered her a growing reputation and acquainted her with many friendly admirers. Winters was on-board now, always on the scavenge for leftover paint to bring home to Elva. A small gallery in Halifax had exhibited some of her work, albeit to derision in the press that such childish images could be considered art. Those who admired Elva's work differed. Often her visitors left with a painting. Sometimes they asked, Are you the girl of the fountain? Always they left wondering, Why don't you speak?

Winters never imagined that he could charge people to stick their head inside the house to see the mess she'd made of things. It allowed him to forgive Elva for what happened with his mother-in-law's place. Long before Rilla's bizarre death, Amos's relatives appeared from St. Stephen and said no way would he have left property to a Mi'kmaq and she'd better stop calling herself his missus. Rilla feared the courts, certain she'd lose her home. Thank God, she'd say to Elva, that justice in this province is like maple sap in a cold spring. Rilla, never legally the wife of Amos Stearns, was not ruled by the courts the unlawful owner of the house at Kirchoffer Place until after her death. Looked like the five hundred dollars was all Winters could expect.

He was eventually compensated, however, with the full jar of silver her art brought in, buried underneath the back stoop. Happy enough, in fact, that he often feared Ol' Noddie might one day float to heaven, or possibly hop a bus to Halifax. Winters would dig up the dollars every so often, count them and bury them without Elva knowing. Insurance.

Winters's property abutted a large parcel of Crown land wedged beside the Demerett town limits. By 1970, Demerett, owing to tourism, looked to expand. The land was viewed for development, you know, golf course, swimming pools, houses mere mortals could never hope to afford—until the Mi'kmaq community said no way. They'd been hunting and fishing on that land for generations. They cited a 1759 treaty.

The sale went forward indifferently. Over a period of months, the standoff between town and native community escalated from name-calling in editorials to threats to highway barricades. The premier ordered the provincial police to reopen roads and restore order. Miscommunication further escalated and shots were threatened before sanity prevailed.

It was first suggested in an editorial in *The Mail-Star*

that Brother Dom, long reclusive, mediate the conflict. He came from the area, might understand local native issues, and was a man of God. The only problem was that Brother Dom refused to be involved in secular matters. Particularly public ones.

It took several months of persuasion from almost every segment of the community and the threat of violence to change his mind. While no one had as yet been hurt, the unresolved issue was likely to become explosive. Only after a personal plea from the premier, the mayor of Demerett and Mi'kmaq leaders did Brother Dom reluctantly agree.

IT WAS MID-AUGUST. The windows in the tiny house were open to the salt air. The brown and orange of black-eyed Susans twitched by the sills, like naughty children peeking inside.

Winters was standing at the doorway, counting and cursing the cars as they came and went. The blocked road and lack of tourists, the tent fringed with flapping sides like those used for garden parties and bigger than their house, no one to buy Elva's paintings or look inside the house — all of it was hurting. How much longer was this to go on?

"It's the goddamned Indians' fault," he said, more to himself than to Elva. "Why not claim the whole fuckin' country for huntin' and fishin'?" Then he turned from the door and pointed at her. "That's what they want, you know. Won't be satisfied until they've got the whole fuckin' Jesus lot and then we won't even be allowed to speak English any more. Those city bastards better not cave in to them."

Elva was painting a winter scene. They sold well in the summer, as summer ones did in the winter. Who knew why tourists wanted what they did?

"They never said anything 'bout closing the road. We're losing trade, Ol' Noddie." And why for Christ's sake did they have to hold that goddamned meeting right next door? "It's not right. Not right."

She glanced up when someone outside yelled. Looking through the open door, past where Winters blocked her view, she watched men rush out of the tent, looking as if they were carrying someone. They appeared confused and stood by the road until Elva heard, There, over there! Then, ten, fifteen, maybe more men in white shirts with sweat stains, some with ties and jackets looking very uncomfortable, others with cameras and tape recorders, raced towards them.

A man had fainted under the stifling air of the big top. The cabin with the droopy flowers on the door seemed just the place to recover. Winters was hustled out of the way. It all happened so quickly and it wasn't just any man.

"Put him down there!"

"Feet up, get his feet up!"

Someone was standing in front of Elva, asking for water. She pointed to the teddy bear on the shelf by the window.

"Here, give him a drink."

Winters stood gaping at the visitor. Someone was apologizing to him for the intrusion.

Elva couldn't see for those around her. She carefully laid down her tray and, with some difficulty, stood. She had expected him to have altered over the decades as she had, but not to the degree she found. His hair, growing in patches from his scarred scalp, was white. He eschewed the dress of the Franciscans, never having actually taken orders, and wore a golf shirt and black trousers.

"Give him some air, let him breathe."

"Has someone gone for an ambulance?"

By now the tiny house was surrounded. Questions were being asked. No one heard answers. Where was the doctor?

"We need to clear the place out, give him some air!"

Someone official, or just acting that way, began ushering everyone outside on orders of the young

Franciscan, Brother Rafe, who appeared to be the man's aide.

"C'mon, c'mon, give the man some privacy."

Winters was saying it was his house. Yes, yes, but they ushered him out as well.

Elva was in the corner.

"You'll have to leave," Brother Rafe instructed her.

So Elva joined the others outside under the hot sun. No one appeared to know what was happening, how the old man was or how this might affect negotiations. Winters was howling about compensation to anyone who'd listen. It would be some time before anyone noticed Elva melting lopsided in the heat and understood the significance of this chance encounter.

But it was not lost on her, and she dreaded the instant the connection was made. When it happened, she knew. They stopped talking. They stared. And almost en masse, they rushed towards the girl from the fountain just as the door to her home opened.

"He wants to see her," Brother Rafe announced.

What does this mean? Why? What does he want with her?

"I'm her husband," Winters said, following.

Looking much recovered, but shaken, Brother Dom was sitting up on the weathered horsehair sofa that was also Elva's bed. The shutters over the small window had been closed, but the brightness of day filtered through the slats to illuminate the walls with a deeper, more thoughtful richness. Evidently, her images had caught his attention.

Winters was his usual self. "Well, sir, you like them? She paints them though you'd not think it by lookin' at her. Can sell you a piece if you're partial to it. Cut it right out if you want. Something to drink, sir, tea, maybe something a bit more powerful—Oh, excuse me, your holiness, you being a man of God and all, not meanin' no disrespect."

"Leave us," he said. "Both of you."

"I don't think that's wise."

The old man was silent. Brother Rafe capitulated.

Well that doesn't seem right, Winters protested, but the ensuing icy silence from so important a visitor reluctantly forced him out on the tail of his opinions. "I'll be right outside this door, Ol'—my dear, if you need me."

Alone, Dom graciously gestured for her to sit back among her paints and geraniums in the corner. The panels, hundreds of miniature voices in every colour shouting from the walls, from the ceiling, from the floor, Come back to us! One side of his face unaltered, the other like it had melted. Standing, he retrieved his cane and hobbled, gazing intently at the pictograms, sometimes lightly brushing his fingertips over them, hearing them. Yes, yes, he said occasionally.

For almost a full half-hour he studied the walls and then he paced out the floor. His hand went up to his heart as if the panels had magic to inflict pain. He shook violently, groaning like a wounded dog, dropping his cane. Elva saw a tear in his right eye, the one not melted. She reached down for his cane.

"The only miracle in this town is that the likes of you could create this wonderful . . . vision of hell."

She rose stiffly and went to him, to steady him. He nodded and took her gnarled hands into his, kissing them.

He gestured to the panels. "We've watched those fools build a miracle on falsehoods and deceit and profit from it, haven't we, Elva?"

She nodded.

"So much time wasted. And I've not said their names in over forty years. Not since, not since —" He winced.

Go, you're free now.

He smiled. "You thought I was Gil hiding in Dom's world."

Once. Yes.

"There hasn't been a moment in all this long life that I haven't wished I was in that grave."

Do they wait in your dreams too? This was said by wiping away his tear.

He thought she meant to silence him. "No, no, hear me, Elva. Let me make it right. Hear the truth, while I've courage."

Look around you. See the truth.

"Elva, I'm still Catholic enough to fear hell. Be my confessor?" She nodded, shyly. "Jane. There. I've said it. Jane! Jane, my Jane. She begged me to take her to the Abbey, our Abbey. That's where she told me about Gil. That she couldn't hate him for what he'd done. And the baby, his."

Tears streamed down one side of his face.

"I blamed her, blamed him. I wanted the pain to go away. And then he showed up. My own brother! My own self. The gun to keep her safe, it just went off. I shot them both. I didn't mean it, Elva. They never knew that about Jane. The baby, it was too late to do anything. It just happened, you must believe that. Then that damned dog of his almost tore me apart. I panicked. That's when I stumbled across the tool shed and the gasoline. I just wanted to make everything seem like an accident. Only it went all wrong. When I got back to shore, the monks found me and gave me this life. Believe me, Elva, no prison sentence could have punished me more."

Dom watched Winters, strutting and muttering, through the shutters. The press perched like shit hawks on the wharf waiting for someone to empty the chum bucket.

"Then there was that idiot John who started everything else, thinking that an old fountain and rain was some kind of miracle. Christ, it rains here all the time!"

They both managed a smile at that.

"And somehow that hound of Gil's survived. Goddamn it, but I watched you and that dog every morning for nine years and 226 days sit by his grave outside my window. Even watched you bury the thing by him when you thought no one noticed. That's how I knew you knew I wasn't Gil. God help me, Elva. The only thing I've regretted all these years is that I didn't say, when they found me, I was him."

Dom started to shake again. Elva opened her arms and he went to her. That's how Brother Rafe found them.

"Seems a shame to cover 'em up," April said as more of the walls succumbed.

Winters's women were like months: May, June and now this one, April. He dipped into a can of white paint.

"That's none of your business. Besides, she won't say nothing, never heard Ol' Noddie speak a word. Well, not since after the good Lord poked her in the head."

"Never?"

"Christ, woman, you deaf too?"

April was still being broken in, so she didn't know much. In that sweaty time in the loft after he'd gone at her like he was jacking up a Dodge Ram, he'd explained about Elva in the fountain.

A few more feet of wall went silent.

"You'll see, Noddie, ol' girl. You can put in some of those spruce trees, like you like them. You won't even miss 'em, startin' all over again. Just paint 'em like I says this time."

Elva stared expressionlessly at the movement of the roller. The vibrant colours were bleeding quickly through the first coat of whitewash. It was going to take two, maybe even three coats.

"Hope that paint dries quickly."

April stretched by the stove, scratched her under-arm. "Will she do new ones?"

"She'll do 'em. That's all she's good for." Although she hadn't painted a thing since the old man had visited. Winters finished rolling over the last of the walls. "That right, Noddie, ol' girl?" he said loud, like she was hard of hearing.

"C'mon, Harry, honey." It didn't bother April that she was about to screw another woman's husband right under her nose, not after she'd seen Elva. Poor guy by rights ought to be allowed a pity fuck.

"Just a quick poke, woman, while this dries. Gotta get more paint up before I lose the light." Winters again snuck a peek at Elva.

"They were kinda pretty, you know, like kids drew 'em. All those fancy home magazines are full of that stuff. Pay big money for that now."

"I ain't going to be out o' pocket, if you catch my drift," Winters said with a tap to his forehead.

Thanks to the Church, guessed Elva. In all the years they'd been married Elva's only value to her husband had been her contribution to his household accounts. Then Brother Rafe returned when Domenique Barthélemy died, three months after mediating the land crisis, and Winters was truly awed by Elva. Imagine that young fellow saying, Name your price, Mr. Winters, to cover up that abomination of hers. Neither Elva nor Winters had any idea what an abomination was, but safe to say, it couldn't be good. And for the money, Winters didn't care.

"You know I was right to do it. It'll bring us something for our keep, woman, maybe extra too."

Winters handed Elva his can of paint, but her swollen hand couldn't bear the weight. No matter, said Winters. You know, at times, he could imagine himself being right kind to her. He smiled at that, his breath tobacco-heavy, teeth yellowed from the habit. Then he patted Elva's head before he followed April up the narrow stairs.

Blacks and reds were first to puncture through the veil. Blues, and Rilla's favourite, yellow, followed. Another wash with white would take care of that.

Afterword

With the death of Elva's widower in 1977, their one-
room home, having fallen into disrepair, vanished.
Considered lost, its fate would remain unknown for the
next quarter of a century while Elva Twohig-Winters's
artistic reputation, as well as the legend of her fabu-
lously painted cedar cottage, steadily grew.

When the house was discovered hidden in a
farmer's shed, it was considered a major find, although
it was in pieces and had been subjected to vandalism,
rain seepage, exposure to salt air and vermin. Much of
it was feared ruined.

Purchased by the Province of Nova Scotia, the
pieces were loaded onto a flatbed truck and taken to a
shopping mall, where the public watched conservators
painstakingly restore the artist's unique voice to its orig-
inal condition. Upon completion, the three- by three-
and-a-half metre house was reconstructed in a specially
designed gallery, the centrepiece of a permanent exhibit
simply titled "Miss Elva."